# AMBUSH IN THE ALLEGHENIES

by

William P. Robertson & David Rimer

ISBN  978-0-7414-4777-7

*Published by:*

INFINITY
PUBLISHING.COM

*Info@buybooksontheweb.com*
*www.buybooksontheweb.com*
*Toll-free  (877) BUY BOOK*
*Local Phone (610) 941-9999*
*Fax  (610) 941-9959*

*Printed in the United States of America*

*Printed on Recycled Paper*

*Published  October 2012*

# CONTENTS

1. CAPTURED ............................................... 1
2. SCOTTISH IRE ......................................10
3. WILL CUTLER .......................................16
4. FRAZER'S PLACE ...................................22
5. MEETING WASHINGTON........................31
6. WINTER CAMP .......................................40
7. MAC'S STORY .........................................47
8. AN AMBUSH GONE AWRY ....................56
9. LOGSTOWN ............................................65
10. THE FRENCH INVASION ........................73
11. A TOUGH JOURNEY ..............................79
12. WILL'S CREEK ........................................86
13. AN EASY VICTORY ................................93
14. A WORSE DEFEAT ................................100
15. THE RING HUNT ...................................108
16. THE GAUNTLET ....................................116
17. HEAD FOR THE RIVER .........................127
18. SAVING BRIGHT STAR .........................133
19. BRADDOCK'S FOLLY .............................145
20. WILL THE WARRIOR .............................156
21. ISHUA TOWN ........................................164
22. WILL'S WEDDING .................................171

BIBLIOGRAPHY ................................................178

# ACKNOWLEDGMENTS

The authors would like to thank the following French & Indian War reenactors for their participation in this project: Dave Bybee, Captain of Marines Du Contrecoeur; Joshua Mihalick, Sergeant of Marines Du Contrecoeur; Bob Houben, Eastern mountain man; John Stengel, Scottish reenactor; Jerry Roberts, Land Pirate Trading Company; Joseph Rearick, Delaware reenactor; and James Selander, www.thequartermastergeneral.com.

A special thanks goes out to Dale Luthringer of Cook Forest State Park, Cooksburg, PA, where most of the photos were taken during their 2007 French & Indian War reenactment. The event is scheduled each year during the first weekend in June. Kudos are also due Missy Clark of Barkertown Sutlers for helping with the details of Scottish emigration. Visit her at www.barkertownsutlers.com.

Finally, the authors would like to acknowledge David Cox who painted the cover of Ambush in the Alleghenies. David is a prize-winning freelance artist from Bradford, PA, and an accomplished teacher of art and martial arts. He also illustrated William P. Robertson's poetry collections 1066, Hearse Verse, and The Illustrated Book of Ancient, Medieval & Fantasy Battle Verse.

The photos in this book were taken by William P. Robertson. He also created The Alleghenies Circa 1755 map on his computer. Robertson's author photo was shot by Dr. Robert Krall. David Rimer's author photo was taken by his wife, Marcia.

# INTRODUCTION

In the 1700's the upper Ohio Valley was a priceless jewel coveted by French voyageurs, English colonists, and several Indian nations. In 1748 Governor Dinwiddie and a select group of Virginia speculators formed the Ohio Company to secure tracts of land and encourage settlement of what was to become Western Pennsylvania. Similarly, the French were moving from Canada and building forts along strategic waterways to lay claim to the region.

Alarmed by this military activity, Dinwiddie sent young George Washington in the fall of 1753 to deliver a letter to the French trespassers. Washington enlisted the help of Christopher Gist as a guide and interpreter for his arduous trip. After many weather-related delays, Washington was able to deliver the governor's message just as winter made travel next to impossible in the primordial wilderness.

The French rejected Dinwiddie's impudent demand that they withdraw from the Ohio Valley, prompting a military response that set ablaze the Alleghenies. It is against this backdrop that four daring trappers get snared in the conflict soon to be known as the French and Indian War. Their story is typical of other brave pioneers who ventured into the dense woods of Western Pennsylvania—a place inhabited by savage men of both European and Native American ancestry.

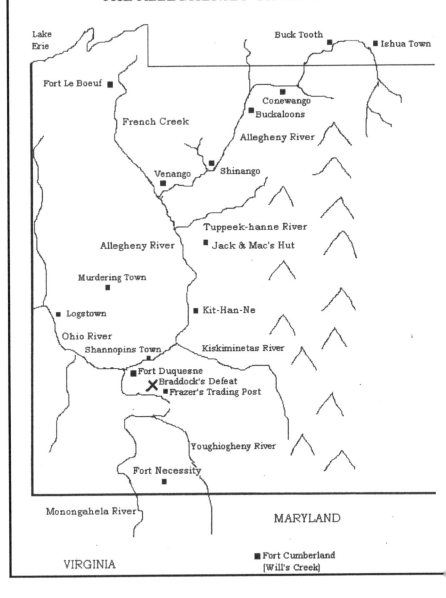

# THE ALLEGHENIES CIRCA 1755

Lake
Erie

Buck Tooth

Ishua Town

Fort Le Boeuf

Conewango
Buckaloons

French Creek

Allegheny River

Venango        Shinango

Tuppeek-hanne River

Allegheny River        Jack & Mac's Hut

Murdering Town

Logstown

Kit-Han-Ne

Ohio River
Shannopins Town        Kiskiminetas River

Fort Duquesne
Braddock's Defeat
Frazer's Trading Post

Youghiogheny River

Fort Necessity

Monongahela River        MARYLAND

VIRGINIA        Fort Cumberland
[Will's Creek]

# CHAPTER ONE: CAPTURED

Black clouds hovered above an endless track of hemlock, oak, and beech. Mist circled hilltops and gathered in ravines, obscuring the woods and making the landscape more ominous. Rain fell in sheets to blot out the whimper of beasts cowering in laurel thickets and labyrinths of vines. Gloom prevailed everywhere in the Alleghenies.

Through the middle of this forebidding land coursed a swollen, roaring river. A tiny canoe made of elm bark fought desperately upstream against the foaming current. It was powered by two young trappers dressed in drenched buckskin. The men's sinewy muscles strained as they dug their paddles into the clear, cold water. Accelerated heartbeats provided the rhythm for their labor.

"I reckon we caught us a panther by the tail this time, Mac," puffed the fellow in the bow as his darting, dark eyes searched for snags and boulders that could rip the bottom from their fragile craft. Often, he thrust his paddle into the churning flood to stave off disaster.

"But our trip will be worth it when we reach Venango," replied the somber Scot, who knelt in the stern of the canoe. "Me possibles bag is so empty, there's not but two round balls rollin' in the bottom. Can't be long now, Jack."

A sudden gust of wind tore at the Scotchman's wool tam, almost blowing it into the river. With a curse, he secured it over his sodden, reddish hair and then paddled even more furiously. His effort sent the canoe surging around a hemlock-choked point. With a few more strokes he was able to see a smaller stream spilling into the river from the north. Where the two waters intersected sat a familiar trading post up on the bank. The crude building was made of mud-chinked logs that would provide welcome shelter for the two soaked trappers. Before Mac could relish this thought, he saw that a palisade was under construction around the hut. A crew of workers scurried about hoisting stakes into gaps in the wall and hammering them into place. Even more disturbing was the white flag etched with gold fleur-de-lis that whipped on a pole near the landing.

"Wagh!" howled Jack Hawkins above the roaring wind. "The Frenchies are turnin' Frazer's place into a fort."

"It's too late to turn back," grunted Alexander MacDonald, pausing to flex his tight forearms. "Sure hope those troops are in a tradin' mood. We're in mighty bad need o' supplies."

"Now, I'm glad we only brung two packs of furs from our cache," mumbled Jack. "Who knows how it'll go with these weasels?"

With worry etched on their tanned faces, MacDonald and Hawkins dug for shore. As they glided up to the dock, four marines dressed in sky-blue waistcoats and black tri-corner hats raced toward them pointing their muskets.

"Out of ze canoe, monsieurs," ordered a sick looking lieutenant through quivering lips. "You are trespassing on the land of Louis XV, King of France."

"We want to see John Frazer," barked Hawkins, springing from the craft with such quickness that he almost capsized his partner into the river. "He'll tell you we's regular customers here."

"We run this Frazer off with all ze English dogs," snarled the officer.

"Then, we want to see the man in charge," demanded MacDonald, crawling onto the dock.

Mac's insolence caused a marine sentry to step forward and smack the Scot with his gun barrel. When Alexander drew himself to his full height, he towered over his assailant like he was a mere boy. He fixed the guard with his flint gray eyes, and the fellow pulled back his musket like he had just wakened a timber rattler with it.

"Thes way, then," wheezed the lieutenant. "Captain Joncaire will be just as glad as me to arrest you."

"Arrest us for what?" snapped Mac.

"For spying!" exclaimed the short sentry, peering out from behind the officer.

"It don't take no spy to see what you're doin' here," guffawed Jack. "Any fellow with two eyes can watch ya work. Why, even a blind man could hear ya hammerin' halfway down the valley."

"Shut up, Anglais, unless you want ze same medicine I give your partner."

"I didn't see ya give him no scent fer our traps. That's the only medicine we's interested in."

"Oui, fermez la bouche!" shrieked the lieutenant, infuriated by Hawkins' quips. "Allez! Allez!"

Jack and Mac took long strides up the dock with the soldiers nipping at their heels like pesky terriers. Both trappers were well over six feet tall and walked with the easy gait of men used to long hikes on the ridge tops. As they stomped along, they noted a fleet of Indian canoes drawn up on the beach to their left. The boats had been turned upside down to keep them from filling with rainwater.

Several Indian boys were cleaning fish near the canoes. One of them kept staring at the two prisoners until MacDonald returned his gaze. Upon noting the lightness of the lad's skin, Alex muttered, "Look at that fellow, Jack. He's a bit pale to be an Ottawa, don't ye think?"

"Allez! Allez!" sputtered the French officer. "And no talking."

"That's like tellin' the wind not to blow," sassed Hawkins, drawing a push from the short marine private behind him.

Jack stumbled from the guard's shove and almost fell on his face. When he had regained his balance, he stared off into the distance to locate a hideous howling that the shifting wind brought to his ears. Behind the half-finished palisade he saw the rest of the Indians whooping like demons in a makeshift camp they had erected. The red men danced and lurched around a huge bonfire, hoisting brown jugs to their lips.

The French prodded their prisoners to the cabin inside the unfinished fort. Ripping open the door, the trappers broke for the roaring fireplace. Hawkins and MacDonald turned their backs to the blaze and let the heat steam dry their soaked clothes. Readjusting the long knives and hatchets in their belts, the men glowered at their captors and spit tobacco juice on the dirt floor. They saw that the cabin was now a military storehouse loaded with stacks of muskets and boxes of rations. Bunks lined the walls where blankets, steel hatchets, and other trade goods had once been shelved. Kegs of rum replaced the ale served only to white men by John Frazer.

A smartly dressed officer with an upturned moustache rose from a steaming plate of venison and bellowed to his lieutenant, "Mon Dieu! What surly fellows are these?"

"Two English spies, Captain Joncaire. And insolent swine to boot."

"Then, they must be sent to Montreal," screeched Joncaire. "Get them out of here before they stink up ze whole barracks."

"Now, hold on there," protested Mac, his face flushing with anger. "Who says we're sided with the English? I hate them even more than you after they slaughtered me kin at Culloden. Ye must have heard o' the massacre and the bloody author of it, the dastard Duke o' Cumberland. I'm a Scot, through and through, and am allied with no redcoat butcher."

"And what about you, fellow?" asked the captain, gesturing to Hawkins with an air of disdain.

"Wall now, I'm Lightnin' Jack Hawkins, I am. A free trapper by trade. I ain't used to takin' orders from no fellow, lobster back or Frenchie. I only come here lookin' to trade some furs fer a little powder an' shot. An' maybe a cup o' rum or two if yer heathens ain't guzzled it all."

"Then, you're not here to spy on our fort?" queried Joncaire with raised eyebrows.

"What fort?" guffawed Jack, scratching at the tangled black beard that made him look much older than his twenty years. "Why, I figgered you was buildin' a pen to keep yer drunk Indians in."

Fighting back a smile, the captain reexamined the rough, simple countenances of the lean woodsmen drying themselves at his hearth.

5

Finally, he said, "These men seem harmless to me, Lieutenant. You may release them. Their freedom, though, comes at a price. Did you see the furs Monsieur Hawkins said they had?"

"Yes, sir," replied the other officer. "They're in his canoe with two long rifles."

"Well then, seize the furs and canoe in the name of our glorious king. Ze rifles they may have, after we relieve them of their black powder. Without powder, the guns will be useless to these bumpkins."

Before Hawkins and MacDonald could protest, the door burst open and in strode an angry Ottawa chief. The chief's head was shorn of all but a scalp lock decorated with feathers, ribbons, and dyed deer hair. His face was fierce even without war paint, and around his neck hung a string of wolf claws. A cape made of wolf hide was draped around his powerful shoulders. Deerskin breeches, decorated with fringe and beadwork, covered his stout legs.

When the chief spied the two trappers, an evil glint flickered in his dark eyes, and his lips curled into a snarl. After plucking at Alexander's red hair, he grunted in guttural French, "Why not told of English captives? Ottawa get scalps of all enemies."

"These men aren't enemies, Bold Wolf," answered Joncaire in his native tongue. "They're merely trespassers."

"One and same. If take beaver, take life of Ottawa. Give me these English to burn with hot splinters. As sign of faith."

"No, I just freed these men," answered the captain carefully. "I cannot go back on my word without losing honor. Do you understand?"

"Me only know French promise guns for war but give rum that weaken for fight. Bold Wolf will shoot English like one pigeon and drive back across water from where came with disease and Walking Purchase. How can white man walk thirty more miles than fastest Delaware in one-and-a-half suns then claim hunting grounds as his own? I spit on them who steal land from our Delaware brothers."

"Soon, there'll be plenty of scalps for all allies of the French king. But not these. That's final."

Besides "shoot English like one pigeon," Hawkins understood little of the conversation between Bold Wolf and Joncaire. What he did recognize was the way the Ottawa kept fingering the scalp knife that hung in a sheath suspended around his neck. Seeing how the red man kept eyeing his thick mane of hair, Lightnin' yanked his coonskin cap down over his ears. Then, with an unflinching glare, he stared down Bold Wolf until the chief turned on his heels and stormed from the barracks. When he had gone, Hawkins whispered to Mac, "Better watch yer topknot while that rascal's around."

"Aye, laddie, an' I'll watch yourn for good measure."

"What did you say?" wheezed the lieutenant.

"Nothin'," grinned Lightnin'. "We was only commentin' on yer fine French hospitality."

"And that is about to end," assured Joncaire, again speaking in English. "Lieutenant, get these hunters their rifles and escort them from camp."

"And what about their furs?" asked the other officer.

"Stash them in the powder magazine. I don't want beaver plews stinking up my bunk like these fellows have."

"Yes, sir," replied the lieutenant, drawing a sword that he used to motion the trappers toward the door. "Allez! Vite!" he commanded. "I must show you ze trail leading south before it is too dark to see. Once you're on it, do not return. Ever!"

"Show us the trail?" echoed Jack with a bemused smirk. "Considerin' how me an' Alex helped blaze it, I reckon we could find it with or without you wavin' that toad stabber."

"Aye, we know every path in the Alleghenies," added MacDonald with a sarcastic laugh as he slipped into his pocket an ingot of lead and a bullet mold that Frazer must have left on the mantel during his expulsion. "We'll be glad to get you Frenchies lost on any one o' them."

Dave Bybee and Josh Mihalick portray French marines like the ones stationed at Venango.

# CHAPTER TWO: SCOTTISH IRE

The first glimmer of dawn was still a half-hour away when Jack and Mac broke cover and crept toward the French fort. With their empty long rifles slung over their shoulders, they moved silently as shadows, pausing every few steps to check the walls ahead for sentries. A light rain deadened their footfalls as they slunk along. They reached the palisade unchallenged and slipped through a gap in the unfinished wall.

Inside, where flickering torches lighted the grounds, the trappers saw two soldiers asleep on their feet near the barracks door. Another guard napped by an outbuilding the men figured was the powder magazine. The blood gushed to MacDonald's face when he recognized this sentry as the same fellow who had hassled him on the dock. Angrily, Mac rushed the dozing Frenchman and whacked him over the head with the flat of his hatchet. Alexander hit him with such force that the sound of the blow resounded across the compound. When no one yelled out after the brief, noisy scuffle, the trappers dragged their victim, legs-first, inside the shed and closed the door behind them.

"Sorry for me rashness, laddie," whispered Alex once they were safe inside. "Me Scottish ire got the best o' me."

"If you hadn't thumped him, I woulda," chortled Hawkins. "There's our furs 'xactly where Joncaire told his lackey to put 'em. An' look at them kegs o' black powder."

"That's mighty convenient," replied Mac-Donald, bending to fill his empty powder horn. "Give me your horn. Quick!"

"I wonder if the Frenchies have breakfast waitin' fer us, too," snickered Jack. "I'm so hungry I could eat what turkey buzzards wouldn't pick at."

"Shhh!" cautioned Mac. "Is that voices I hear?"

Alexander cracked open the door to find the French lieutenant reaming out the sleepy barracks guards. He gestured angrily and vilified his men until their shoulders drooped like their soggy moustaches. The little rooster was so busy exerting his authority that he never once glanced toward the powder magazine. Finally, the lieutenant ordered the disgraced soldiers inside to face Captain Joncaire.

After the French disappeared into the barracks, Jack and Mac grabbed their furs and long rifles and stole back across the compound. With their hearts in their throats, they tiptoed along, expecting any second to be spotted. When they safely reached the fort gate, they exchanged nervous grins and stepped outside. It was now just getting light, so the woodsmen hurried down to the dock where their canoe was still tied up from the night before.

"Won't be long now before the Frenchies find that other guard," grunted Mac as they secured the furs in the bottom of their craft.

"An' even that dunderhead lieutenant will figger we's the author o' this mischief once he sees our canoe's gone," Hawkins said.

"Then, why don't we even up the odds a little?" suggested Alex with a playful gleam in his eye.

"An' how do we do that?"

"Ram our knives through the bottom of their canoes is how. Me Scottish ire demands it after that heathen chief eyed me like a fatling calf."

"No, that'd make so much noise, we'd wake them drunk Ottawas. Let's chuck their paddles in the river instead. That'll slow 'em down."

"Let's do it!"

The trappers streaked for the beach to fish inside the overturned canoes. Feverishly, they gathered the stashed paddles, lugged them to the river, and slipped them one-by-one into the flood. They had just watched the last of them float off downstream when a hair-raising howl more befitting a beast than a man echoed down the bank behind them.

Lightnin' whirled to see the incensed Bold Wolf, with the help of the light-skinned Indian boy, herding a band of retching warriors toward the river. The sick Ottawas stumbled and staggered along, holding their stomachs and hoping a dip in the cold water would help their misery. Only the chief was armed. He threw a musket to his shoulder even before his war cry had spread alarm into the fort. His aim was thrown off when the lad stumbled and bumped into him as he pulled the trigger.

Hawkins flinched as a puff of white smoke burst from the end of Bold Wolf's rifle. In the next instant he was sprinting toward his canoe with Alexander loping along several yards behind. By then, a steady stream of soldiers was spewing from Venango to unleash a hail of bullets that whined and whizzed past the streaking trappers. As they skidded up the slippery dock, one ball clipped the coon tail from Lightnin's cap and another sang off the stock of his unloaded gun.

The fusillade grew even more intense when Hawkins and MacDonald reached their canoe. As Mac bent to slip into his usual place in the stern, several bullets burrowed through his loose-fitting buckskin shirt, barely missing his ribs. Jack, meanwhile, cut the mooring rope with one desperate whack of his hatchet. With bullets chasing him like bees, he dove into the bow of the already moving canoe.

Alexander was paddling like mad before Jack could right himself. The bullets now raised plumes of water all around them as Bold Wolf and the cursing Frenchmen raced onto the dock to fire several more volleys. The other Indians, meanwhile, charged for their beached canoes. The exertion made many of them vomit, and their retching mixed with keening wails of disappointment when they found their paddles missing.

Hawkins and MacDonald doubled their exertion until they finally shot out of rifle range. Then, they worked their way downriver through a long, deep pool with Bold Wolf and the French giving chase along the bank. They didn't slow their paddling until they hit the first chute of rapids. When the mighty current whipped them along faster than their pursuers could run, Mac shouted, "We beat them rascals, curse their hides."

"Now, we can set back an' enjoy the ride," whooped Lightnin'.

"Aye, if ye call steerin' through this white water hell a good time," yelped the Scotchman.

"Wall now, it sure do beat anything them Ottawas had planned for us," reminded Jack, fending off a rock that loomed suddenly from the foaming flux. "Keep a close eye now."

The canoe shot along at breakneck speed with the two trappers howling with fear and exhilaration. Several times their craft shot clear out of the water, while twice it came close to capsizing. Through every crisis Mac guided them back on course until the torrent spit them into another long pool.

"Now, I see why we portaged them rapids on the way upstream," croaked Lightnin'. "I ain't had that much fun since I broke through the beaver pond ice on a twenty below day."

"Well, we beat the river this time," gasped a very pale Alex. "After that ride, I'm not so sure I'd call it 'La Belle Riviere' like the Frenchies do."

"No, I pre-fer its Indian name, 'Alleghenny.' That's got some menace to it."

"You mean just like everything we face out here in the frontier."

"An' I wouldn't have it no other way!" exclaimed Jack.

The rain had finally quit falling, and the trappers paddled along staring at the wilderness that hemmed them in on both sides of the river. Dominating the landscape were hemlocks that towered over a hundred feet tall. The Allegheny provided the only sure road through this impenetrable forest, which also included great stands of oak, hickory, maple, and beech. In the presence of such majesty, the men's voices fell to hushed whispers.

MacDonald and Hawkins continued downriver until they reached the familiar territory of their hunting grounds marked by some massive oak and a burned-over meadow. There, they ran aground on a fine gravel beach and splashed ashore. Glancing around them with trepidation, they immediately lugged their canoe into the undergrowth. Turning it upside down beneath a fallen log, they concealed it further with dead leaves and branches. When they had finished their task, Lightnin' said, "With the woods crawlin' with hostiles, this here canoe could come in handy again."

"Aye," agreed Mac. "If we ever get in a fix, we can always beat it back here an' take to the river."

"Sure as a gun has hind sights," uttered Hawkins. "Speakin' o' which, I reckon we best load our rifles before we take another step. Mighty generous o' them Frenchies to supply us with all that free powder. I jess wish I had more 'n' two round balls to go with it."

With a broad grin, Alex reached in his pocket and produced the ingot of lead and the bullet mold he had filched from the French barracks. "Once we get to our supply cache and fetch our iron pot, we can cast all the balls we need," beamed the Scotchman. "Let's go before it gets too dark to find our way there."

"An' we best start huntin' fer a fat deer," suggested Jack. "We ain't et in two days, an' my belly's rumblin' like a Conestoga wagon on a corduroy road."

"Then, how are we going to sneak up on any game, Lightnin'?"

"Jess like always—one sure step at a time."

# CHAPTER THREE: WILL CUTLER

Jack Hawkins and Alexander MacDonald loaded their rifles, strapped bundles of furs on their backs, and then crept south down the trail that followed the east bank of the Allegheny. The path was only wide enough for them to travel single file through the dense woods. Often, they had to duck branches that intruded across the narrow lane. The incessant autumn rain had turned the path into slippery muck that constantly tested the men's agility.

Lightnin' and Mac hadn't slogged along for more than a quarter-mile when they heard someone skating along the trail behind them. Exchanging alarmed glances, the trappers concealed themselves in the laurel. There, they drew their hatchets and crouched down to spring at the interloper.

A grin flashed in Jack's beard when he spied a gangly boy coming pell-mell down the path. The lad's feet were flying in every direction as he tried to keep his balance on the slick ground. He was dressed in a mud-spattered blanket coat and wore his hair shaved on the sides, Indian fashion. He also wore beaded Ottawa leggings. It wasn't until he was even with Jack's hiding place that he saw the boy was white.

"Hold on thar, young fella, before you falls on your back like an upturned turtle," chortled Lightnin', rising from the brush.

"Aye, what's your hurry?" hissed Mac, grabbing the boy just as his feet flew out from under him. "Why, this is the same lad we seen cleaning fish at Venango."

"S-S-Seein' you's what gave me the courage to r-r-run off," stuttered the boy. "I watched you escape. Then, I t-t-tried it. Let's go!"

"Take it easy," encouraged MacDonald softly. "You're safe with us. I'm Alex, and this here's Jack. We're on our way to our supply cache. After that, we'll see if we can get ye back to your folks."

"Don't have none," sniffed the lad. "The Ottawas. . .killed Father."

"Them dirty skunks!" exclaimed Lightnin'. "We had a tussle with their chief yestiddy ourselves. If I ever run into that Bold Wolf rascal again, we's gonna butt heads like a couple o' bull elk. An' I'll be the one doin' the goring!"

Upon hearing the chief's name, the boy burst into tears and threw his arms around Alexander's neck. When he had cried himself out, the Scot asked him, "What's your name, laddie?"

"Young Hawk."

"I mean your Christian name."

"Um. . .Will."

"Will what?"

"Will. . .Um. . .Will Cutler."

"Well, Will Cutler," said Mac, "we best get movin' again. It'll be dark soon. There's a spring not far from here where we can make camp. We don't have much to share with you 'cept our fellowship."

"Thanks," replied Will with a tearful smile. "That'll be plenty enough. Y-Y-You two look hungry. Here."

The boy pulled a pouch of pemmican from under his coat and offered it to his new friends. Jack and Mac each took a handful of the dried meat and ate greedily as they again headed down the trail. The woods were eerily quiet, and the trappers peered with keen eyes into the underbrush. They also stopped every few steps to listen and sniff the air like beasts.

Finally, the travelers reached a splintered hemlock that had been sheared in half by lightning. There, the men left the trail and began digging with their hands in the soft forest soil until they unearthed a trapdoor made of logs. Beneath the door was a hole in the ground containing a stash of furs and an assortment of other trade goods. They fetched out a knife for Will and the iron pot they needed to cast bullets. They also withdrew a pack of beaver plews for the boy to carry before carefully concealing the remainder of their treasure.

Snapping some hemlock twigs from the trunk of a nearby tree, Mac started a small, hot fire. He added only the driest wood that wouldn't produce telltale smoke. He placed the iron pot on the blaze and dropped an ingot of lead inside. Once the lead melted, he poured some of it into the scissors style bullet mold that Hawkins held by its wooden handles. A few minutes later Jack separated the handles, and a perfect .45 caliber round ball fell into the piece of deerskin he had laid on the ground before him.

"W-W-Why aren't we g-g-going?" stammered the boy impatiently as he watched the two hunters work. "Aren't you afraid the Ottawas will c-c-catch us?"

"We best have enough bullets if they do," whispered the Scotchman with a thin smile.

18

"Now, why don't ye tell us how ye got yourself into this fix."

Tears welled up in Will's blue eyes as the painful memory of his capture reformed in his brain. He sat cross-legged next to Mac and extended his strong, smallish hands over the fire. He had pale cheeks and a square chin. His Indian garb did little to disguise his distinct English features.

A wounded look convulsed Will's face when he chirped in a squeaky, adolescent voice, "Father and I come to America two years ago. There wasn't enough money to pay passage for me mum and six sisters, but we figured we'd earn it soon enough in the New World. Father left England because of the king's taxes. He couldn't feed us kids no matter how many barrel hoops he made."

"Aye, the king steals our money to fight his wars an' live in luxury," raged MacDonald. "Curse King George the Second an' all the bleedin' monarchs!"

"That's why I live out here in the wilderness," chortled Lightnin'. "I gets to keep all I earn an' walk tall an' free. The only royalty in these parts are eagles an' mountain lions. But get on with yer story, Will."

"Yes, please!" interjected Alex. "If Jack starts spinnin' yarns, ye won't get to say another word for a fortnight."

Grinning at Mac's comment, Will continued, "Father worked as a hoop maker in Philadelphia until he earned enough to buy three pack horses and some cloth, knives, and other goods to trade to the Indians for furs. He heard there was big money to be made as a front line trader, but he sure didn't know how hard it would be traveling through the thick woods and over all them mountains."

"I learned the same lesson, laddie," Mac said with a knowing shake of his thick, red mane. "Even the Scottish Highlands didn't ready me for this rough country."

"I also missed me mum," sniffed Will. "Father didn't cook worth a lick and never showed me any. . .love. All them miles we tramped made him as hard as the life we lived. . ."

"Then, he musta been able to handle hisself in a scuffle," observed Jack. "What happened to yer pap, anyhow?"

"Everything was bully while we traded with the friendly Iroquois. We visited lots of their villages like Buck Tooth, Conewango, and Buckaloons. Then, we come down Shinango way and run into a party of strange Indians along the trail. They was mostly braves on a hunting trip. They soon made it clear through hand signs that they wanted rum. Father told them he had none, but they wouldn't believe him. When one devil started rummaging through the packs, my pa grabbed his arm and shoved him away. That was when Bold Wolf stuck his hatchet in the back of Father's head. I'll never forget the look that crossed his face. . . as he fell. . .dead."

"What did ye do then?" asked Alexander. "I saw me own dear father slaughtered by the English at Culloden. I couldn't speak for a whole day after that."

"I just froze. I didn't do anything while I watched my father's killer rip off his scalp. When those heathens tore apart our packs and found no liquor, they whined like dogs. Then, they took me down the Ohio River to their village and adopted me into the tribe."

"Well, you're back among your own now," reminded Mac, patting the boy roughly on the shoulder. "We're done bullet makin' for the day. Let's erase all traces o' our fire an' get out o' here before them Ottawas find us."

"If they do," cried the boy, "I'll stab this knife through Bold Wolf's heart for s-s-striking Father down!"

"Them's powerful words," muttered Lightnin', "but in dealin' with red men, that's the only kind to use. Indians respect brav'ry 'bove all else. Remember that, an' it may save yer life one day."

"Bravery's somethin' this lad's got plenty of," added Mac. "I saw how he saved our topknots by throwin' off Bold Wolf's shot at Venango."

"That took a lot o' sand," agreed Hawkins with a grin. "Now, Will, it's time to see how strong a back ya got."

"Aye, strap on these furs," instructed MacDonald, handing the boy a thick pack of beaver skins. "We need supplies to get through another winter, and ye can help by carrying these plews to Frazer's place."

"An' we best fetch the winter robes from our cache before we hoof it," said Hawkins with a shiver.

"Indeed, we should," answered Alex, glancing warily at the horizon. "If them ain't snow clouds a bilin' in the sky, then I weren't born to me Scottish mother."

# CHAPTER FOUR: FRAZER'S PLACE

"How far we gonna tramp before we get to Frazer's?" croaked Will, collapsing beneath the weight of the furs he carried.

"Wall now, we's only stomped for four days," chuckled Jack. "I reckon we got a might farther to go, bein' John had to build his new tradin' post off French land."

"Why don't we ask this fellow?" suggested Alexander, pointing toward a grizzled trapper who slogged up the trail toward them through the sloppy, wet snow that had fallen overnight.

"I'll be dipped!" exclaimed Hawkins. "It's Bearbite Bob Winslow. I ain't seen him in a coon's age."

"How'd he get that name?" panted the lad as he watched the other woodsman raise his long rifle above his head to salute them.

"By surviving a maulin' that would have killed most fellas. Old Bob's tough as they come. An' he's the best trapper in these parts. He's caught more beaver than the hairs growin' in that tangled beard o' his."

"What's you tellin' this tired Indian boy 'bout me, Lightnin'?" roared Bob, giving Hawkins a bear hug that left Jack gasping for breath.

"Nothin' yer mama wouldn't say," choked Jack. "How ya been, old man?"

"Who you callin' 'old'? Why, I still got the fight o' ten wildcats in me an' the eyes of an eagle."

Reenactor, Bob Houben, portrays an Eastern mountain man. He carries the standard equipment of all free trappers: a long rifle, a powder horn, and a possibles bag.

"Then, why don't ya sprout wings an' fly off to catch us some supper?" wheezed Hawkins.

"That's the Jack I remember," cackled Bob. "Always hungry an' even more ready to out lie any feller he meets along the trail."

"Do ye know how far it is to John Frazer's place?" asked MacDonald, shaking hands with the elder woodsman.

"He's done settled down Turtle Creek way along the Monongahela. Got hisself a dandy location. He's well stocked, too. I just come from there, so I know, personal like."

"Where ya headed this late in the season, Bearbite? I thought you buzzards went into roost long before now," needled Hawkins.

"I figgered I'd winter up Conewango way, away from them Frenchies."

"Well, we best be headin' out. We ain't et nothin' in some time, 'cept the dried meat the boy give us. Did ya leave any game fer us in the woods down yonder?"

"Weren't nothin' movin' back there, Lightnin', but one small doe. The only place she's goin' is down my gullet. I could spare a little venison if ya need some."

"Yes, please," replied Alex. "An' ye best be on your lookout for some Ottawas that are lurking about upriver."

"If they's as tame as this boy here, they shouldn't be no problem."

"They're led by Bold Wolf!" snapped Will, bristling at Winslow's affront. "I learned plenty of nastiness from him."

"Wagh!" yelped Bearbite. "Then, I'll hunt the headwaters o' the Tuppeek-hanne where I'll be safe. Drop by anytime if ya run low on victuals."

24

"Thankee," replied Jack, munching on the roast venison Bob handed him. "Watch yer topknot."

"Watch yourn."

The three travelers waved goodbye to the old-timer and again headed south along the Allegheny. During their trek, the snow changed to rain, then to sleet, and back to snow again. The footing became extremely treacherous, and countless times they slipped on rocks or were tripped by protruding tree roots. The snow plastered the trees, creating a dim tunnel to stumble through. Muddy quagmires made the going even tougher. By late afternoon they'd only covered eight miles.

Finally, the trappers reached the turbulent Kiskiminetas River. When they saw it was too deep to ford, Will groaned, "W-W-What do we do now?"

"We got hatchets, don't we?" replied Jack with a tired grin. "Come morning, we'll fell a tree 'cross them narrows upriver a piece an' make us a dandy bridge."

"Aye, things are never as grim as they seem, laddie," added MacDonald. "We're smarter than the rest o' God's creatures, and they tend to survive."

"Hey, let's build us a lean-to," suggested Hawkins, hacking some branches from a nearby tree. "Then, we'll be snugger than squirrels in a hollow stump. Come help me, Will."

"Sure."

Will and Jack hoisted one end of a fallen log and wedged it into the crotch of a young oak. Next, they tilted poles on either side of the log to form an A-frame roof. They thatched the roof with hunks of bark and pine-needle branches. By the time they finished, Alexander had a roaring fire going and a pot of wintergreen tea on to boil. He also had some cattail roots cooking in the coals. The roots would serve as their supper.

As soon as darkness fell, the exhausted trappers crawled in their shelter and huddled together for warmth. The temperature continued to plunge, forcing Mac to get up around midnight to move their fire directly in front of the hut entrance. The wind shrieked through the black trees, and snow pummeled him as he labored with his task.

By morning the travelers' crude shelter was completely snow-covered and so cozy they hated to leave it. Lightnin' was the first to brave the frigid air, and he whooped for joy as he surveyed the glistening landscape that greeted him. "Git out here," he ordered. "We's gonna make good time today."

"What are ye yappin' about?" grumbled Alexander, sticking his head out the entrance.

"Wall now, you grouchy, old Scot, lookee there. The river done fell a foot. We'll cross her slicker 'n' a beaver can gnaw through birch bark."

"This snow will keep down the mud, too," said Mac with renewed enthusiasm. "Come on, Will. It's time to hoof it."

After the trappers carefully extinguished their fire, they snatched up their belongings and boiled down the bank of the Kiskiminetas River. Cackling like a maniac, Hawkins plunged into the icy, waist-deep water. He plowed through the flood, holding his rifle high over his head. His voice rose several octaves as he urged his friends to follow.

With much splashing and many cold gasps, Jack, Mac, and Will forded the river without incident. When they hit the trail on the other side, they loped along to increase their circulation. Warmed by this exertion, they kept jogging until they reached the intersection of three powerful rivers. Following the watercourse that roared into the others from the south, they never slowed until they saw smoke rising from a cabin that peeked from the distant woods.

"That must be Frazer's now," puffed Hawkins, decelerating to a cautious walk. "Soon, we'll be chawin' down biscuits smothered in goose gravy."

"An' a guzzlin' some bitters if we're lucky," beamed Mac.

"Then, why are we slowing down?" asked Will. "Are you that tired?"

"It's best not to surprise folks livin' in this wilderness," Jack replied, "'less you like eatin' hot lead fer dinner."

The woodsmen grew silent at Hawkins' observation and crept toward the long, log house that was twice the length of the usual cabin and had a chimney built on each end. As they drew closer, they heard guttural voices haggling with an Englishman around front.

Jack signaled for the others to halt and then slipped along the left wall of the cabin. Noiselessly, he stole to the corner to peer at an Indian hunting party gathered around Frazer's shut door. When Cutler and MacDonald's curiosity drew them to Jack's side, they heard the Indian leader, Deep Waters, say, "We want trade prime plew for rifle. Have ten bundle. What say?"

As John Frazer mulled over the offer, Will whispered, "Which tribe are those bucks from?"

"Shawnee," muttered Lightnin'.

"How do ye know that?" asked Mac. "All these red men look alike to me."

"They probably say that 'bout Scotchmen, too. Look at them heavy ear wheels they's wearin'. An' the red lines tattooed on their faces. They's also got buffalo robes that not many tribes 'round here can git."

"I wonder what they're doing this far east?" asked Mac.

"Don't know, but I got a funny feelin' about 'em."

"They don't look so dangerous," countered Cutler. "Are you suspicious of them just because they're Indians?"

"No, that ain't it. I don't like the way them bucks keep edgin' closer to John."

The Shawnees dropped ten thick bundles of furs at Frazer's feet, and the chief repeated his demand for guns.

"Ya know, Deep Waters, the cost is a stack o' furs that's tall as the rifle," said the trader. "You've got four rifles worth o' plews there an' enough left over fer some powder an' lead."

The chief nodded excitedly at John's answer until he added, "Before I fetch out the merchandise, let me take a closer look at them pelts o' yours."

Frazer drew a knife from the sheath he wore on a thong around his neck and cut the strap holding together the closest bundle of furs. The first five skins he examined were all prime beaver. When he got to the sixth, though, he discovered an old wolf hide. Below that were inferior fox, raccoon, and muskrat pelts.

"What are you tryin' to pull?" snarled John, looking the chief square in the face.

"If you not give rifles, we take," grunted Deep Waters, drawing his hatchet as a signal to his men.

Before the Shawnees could overpower Frazer and burst inside the trading post, Jack stepped into the open and blared, "Not so fast thar!"

At the sound of Hawkins' voice, a scowling brave whirled to fling his tomahawk at the intruder. Before the 'hawk left the brave's hand, Jack blew it to smithereens with a quick shot from his long rifle. As the Indian yelped in surprise and pain, three of his tribesmen rushed to attack Lightnin' before he could reload his piece. At that moment Mac leaped around the corner and blasted another warrior through the thigh. The other two Indians kept coming, flailing their hatchets and howling like blood-maddened wolves. MacDonald and Hawkins calmly clubbed them to the ground with the butt ends of their guns and then stormed forward to deal with the crowd surrounding Frazer.

John used the diversion to slash Deep Waters across the cheek with his knife. The chief was so grieved by the stinging wound that he dropped his hatchet. By then, Jack and Mac had closed on the other bucks and clubbed them repeatedly until they too surrendered. One of the culprits tried to run off but was tripped up by Will as he disappeared around the corner of the cabin. The boy kicked the Shawnee's tomahawk away and drew the knife Mac had given him. Thus armed, Will threatened the Indian until he rejoined the rest of his defeated band.

"Wall now, Deep Waters, why don't you varmints head down that trail before I gits real upset," snarled Lightnin'.

"Yes, go!" rumbled John, motioning off downriver. "An' take them worthless furs with ya."

Muttering angry threats, the chief signaled for his hunting party to gather their pelts. After fixing Hawkins with an evil glare, the Shawnee led his braves away from the trading post. His steps became more animated as his fury raged within him.

Just before Deep Waters disappeared into the forest, he slipped his bow off his shoulder, drew a deadly flint-pointed arrow, and sent it flying toward Jack. Lightnin' dodged at the last instant, and the missile stuck in the trading post door. It quivered there until the woods swallowed up the coward who had shot it.

"Should we reload an' chase down those rascals?" growled Mac, the blood rushing to his cheeks.

"No, let 'em go," advised Hawkins. "All we'll do is git ourselves ambushed if we follow 'em into that tangle. I reckon we'll git another crack at 'em before all's said an' done."

"Am I glad you fellows come along," choked Frazer, shaking Lightnin's hand. "If ya ever need credit to buy supplies, you got it."

"Wagh! Let go, John," wailed Hawkins. "What do ya do, squeeze rocks inta sand to git yer grip so powerful?"

"No, I do a little blacksmithin' on the side is all. Repair guns an' traps, shoe horses, that sort o' thing."

"Then, you're a mighty 'handy' fellow," laughed Alex. "Hope you're equally good at cooking supper 'cause that's what us boys need most."

# CHAPTER FIVE: MEETING WASHINGTON

The trappers followed Frazer inside the trading post where he seated them before his glowing fireplace. John turned a haunch of venison he had cooking on a spit and then went into the pantry to fetch his guests some corn bread. As Jack, Mac, and Will wolfed down huge hunks of johnnycake, Frazer asked, "Where you boys come from?"

"Up Venango way," answered Hawkins, "where the Frenchies are still buzzin' like bees."

"Those skunks got a lot o' nerve claimin' Ohio Company land."

"An' even more fer pushin' out hardworkin' fellas like you an' me. Hey, how come you ain't got a goose roastin'? I sure had a hankerin' fer a fat drumstick since the last time I ate here."

"Same old Lightnin'," laughed John, "always thinkin' of his belly first. Them geese flew by weeks ago. Must be a hard winter comin'. The deer meat should be about ready. You're welcome to start carvin' on it."

Jack drew his knife and sliced off a steaming chunk of meat. He had barely lifted it to his mouth when the door creaked open and in stomped seven travelers covered with wet snow. The party was led by a tall, muscular frontiersman whose 50 hard years were mapped on the lines of his rugged face. Behind him entered an even taller young man and a scholarly looking gentleman. Four nondescript woodsmen trailed in last.

"If it ain't Christopher Gist," blared Hawkins, addressing the elder woodsman. "Who you towin' in behind ya?"

"Well, thar, Lightnin', none other than Major George Washington."

"An' who's the older chap?"

"That's Jacob Van Braam. The major brung him along to translate when we parley with the French."

"He looks too much like a gent to be trampin' through these woods."

"Don't let his mild appearance fool ya none. He's also quite the fencin' master."

"I didn't think ya needed a teacher to build a fence," joshed Hawkins. "Nice to meet you fellas."

Washington cleared his throat a couple of times at Jack's poor joke and then nodded a reserved hello. At six-foot-three, the major even towered over Lightnin', and his serious demeanor made him seem older than his twenty-one years. There was a look of authority in his steely, gray eyes, and Mac and Will moved aside to let George warm himself before the fire.

"Good to see ya, Major," enthused Frazer, stepping forward to crush Washington's hand in his powerful grip. "It's 'bout time Governor Dinwiddie sent someone to check on them French marines."

"Do you have any coffee?" asked George, deflecting the trader's comment.

"Excuse my manners, sir. I'll get a pot bilin' for ya. Please. Help yerself to the other victuals."

"Thank you, John. We've come a far piece today and are in bad need of some hot food. It snowed the whole way down the Monongahela, and our buckskins are soaked clean through."

"Monongahela?" smirked Hawkins. "Do ya know how that river got its name?"

"It means 'banks fallin' in'," replied Christopher.

"No! No!" corrected Lightnin'. "It's Indian fer 'Shawnee bathe here.' That's why the water's so dirty."

After dinner, George, Gist, John, and Jack sat before the fire smoking their pipes. They kept their voices low so as not to disturb the other guests, who snored in buffalo robe beds on the floor.

"As you guessed earlier, John," whispered Washington, "the governor of Virginia has sent me here to contact the French commandant. His name is General Pierre Paul Sieur de Marin. Ever heard of him?"

"Won't have much luck talkin' to him," answered Frazer. "The general died sudden-like several days ago at Fort Le Boeuf."

"That's on the Allegheny," muttered Gist. "I only know the lower Ohio, havin' surveyed it fer the Ohio Company."

"That can't be right," insisted George. "Being in charge of the Mississippi, too, the French general always stayed farther south."

"No, all them Mississippi soldiers have returned to Montreal fer the winter. That's a thousand mile march."

"Looks like we'll be heading north, then," said the major with determination glittering in his eyes. "I sure hope we get there before winter prevents us from traveling."

"But that ain't the only bad news I got fer ya," mumbled Frazer, handing George a wampum belt made of purple and white beads. "This here's a speech-belt. The Iroquois give it to me to send to Governor Dinwiddie. It says the Chippewas, Ottawas, and Orundacks have gone over to the Frenchies."

"That means war!" yelped Lightnin'.

"And that's something even you can't joke about," grunted the major.

The next morning George Washington rousted his party from their beds at first light. After a hearty breakfast of oatmeal and more johnnycake, Frazer lent the major and Gist a large canoe to take their baggage downstream. The rest of the men headed up the trail north with the horses. As Washington cast off from shore, he barked to Jack, "What we discussed last night must not be told to anyone, including your friends. Is that clear, Hawkins?"

"You don't need to worry none, sir. I musta slept with my ear pointin' at the floor 'cause every one of them words we spoke plumb drained out o' my head."

Jack, Mac, Will, and John waved goodbye to Gist and Washington until the canoe disappeared around a bend in the river. Then, Mac said with a low whistle, "The major sure is all business. That man is a born leader if I ever seen one."

"The only reason you like him is 'cause his hair's as red as yourn," teased Lightnin'. "An' bein' an officer will make his topknot a bigger prize to all them Ottawas, Chippewas, an' Orundacks."

"Now, why are ya tellin' him 'bout them tribes after Washington ordered you not to?" asked Frazer.

34

"If Mac's to keep his scalp, he best know which Indians have sided with the Frenchies. Hey, there's one thing we talked about last night that even the major can't object to me spillin'."

"What's that?"

"Wall, John, it's that trade we made by the firelight. My furs for yer smoke pole. Go fetch it out here, will ya?"

"Sure."

"Smoke pole?" echoed Will. "What's that?"

"Yer very own long rifle is what."

"Really? Why would you buy me a rifle?"

"Ya can't go unarmed if you're goin' a trappin' with me an' Mac."

"Trapping?"

"Unless you'd rather live in England with a house full o' sisters again."

"And miss out on that adventure?" sputtered Cutler. "But how will I ever repay you?"

"With the plews ya trap this winter."

"Aye, laddie, we'll teach ye all the tricks," assured Alexander.

"First, you'll have to show me how to fire my gun."

"Here comes Frazer with her now!" whooped Lightnin'. "Ain't she a beaut? Look at how her barrel's been browned. The sun can't glint off it to warn a bar or Frenchie."

John placed the Pennsylvania rifle in Will's hands, and the boy's eyes traveled up and down the finely crafted walnut stock. He gasped at the beautiful brass patchbox, trigger guard, and butt plate. Although the gun was almost as tall as he was, he threw it to his shoulder and found its fifty-six inches to be perfectly balanced. Finally, he cried, "Thank you so much! Armed with this piece, I'm a real mountaineer like you."

"Not with that Indian hair, you ain't," chuckled Jack. "We best buy ya a coonskin cap 'til yer hair grows back normal-like."

"Will you teach me to shoot, now?" asked the boy, jumping up and down with excitement.

"Only after you settle yourself," said Mac, suppressing a smile. "You'll need a nice calm aim if ye hope to hit anything."

"That an' a proper loaded gun," added Jack. "First off, uncork this here powder horn an' fill the sixty grain powder measure. After ya dump the powder down the barrel, here's a patch to set over the muzzle. Then, put this round ball in the center o' the patch. With the short starter push the ball just far enough down the barrel so ya can cut off the extra cloth with yer patch knife. See, I hang my sheath 'round my neck, so it's always nice an' handy."

"This sure takes a long time," croaked the boy. "If I missed a deer, I'd never get loaded again in time to get another shot."

"It all becomes second nature after ye've done it a thousand times," said Alexander. "Watch carefully while Jack explains the rest o' the process."

"Now, you're ready to ram home the ball," continued Lightnin'. "Use a hand over hand style to put the ramrod down the barrel. That'll keep ya from breakin' it. Keep pushin' 'til ya seat the ball on the powder."

"So are we ready to shoot?" asked Cutler.

"Not quite, Will. Didn't your pa teach ya nothin' 'bout firearms?"

"No, he never bought a gun. He didn't want to alarm the friendly Indians we traded with. The Ottawas only let the warriors have rifles. They did show me a thing or two about bows and arrows. After a while I even outshot their best hunters, so I reckon I can learn this, too."

"Well, then, watch real close like, an' I'll shows ya the last step."

"Yes, sir, Jack."

"Finally, ya need to fill the pan with primin' powder. The pan's right below the lock there. That's it. Now, pull back the hammer, an' you're ready to shoot."

"Why does my rifle have two triggers?" asked Will.

"Oh, I fergot about that. The short one's the set trigger. Ya have to tug on it first before the gun can fire. It acts as a safety, so yer weapon can't go off accidental-like. It also makes the pull o' the actual trigger more smooth."

"I guess I've got it," grinned the boy. "What shall I shoot at?"

"Why not at this here?" suggested Lightnin', crossing the yard to a pile of firewood and holding up a circular log, two-feet in diameter. "I'll set it up 'bout thirty yards to start with. Then, we'll adjust yer sights if ya hit it in the same place twice in a row."

"If ye don't hit it, we'll move it even closer," said Mac. "Now, put your gun to your shoulder an' peer through the back sight until your front sight is centered in the middle o' it. An' squeeze the trigger."

Will did as he was instructed, even remembering to pull the set trigger before lining up his sights. Holding for the middle of the log, he touched off a shot and sent a huge cloud of black powder smoke rolling out the barrel. Hawkins ran to look at the target and then let out a low whistle. "I'll be dipped!" he exclaimed. "The boy done took her clean through the middle."

"Then, move the target back to 50 yards," ordered Mac. "We'll see how he does there."

Will's second shot was equally accurate, so the target was lugged out to one hundred yards. There, he pulled his next bullet high and to the left. When Jack reported the spot, Cutler cried, "Dang! I knew I yanked the trigger that time. Let me shoot one more."

A serious look crossed the lad's face. He took three deep breaths and closed his eyes. Finally, he stared down the sights and squeezed the trigger until the gun surprised him when it went off.

"Another center shot!" hollered Jack upon examining the log.

"Will, let me see that piece o' yours," requested Alex. "No wonder it shoots so good. Look. There's Joel Ferree's name stamped on the barrel. I visited his gunshop in Lancaster County an' seen him personally sight in the rifle he had just built."

"An' there's another good reason fer her accuracy, too," chuckled Jack.

"There is?"

"Sure, Will. Her barrel's been perfectly welded from the middle to the ends to purge her o' devils. Soon, you'll be barkin' squirrels from a tree at 300 yards with her."

"I can't wait!" yelped Cutler.

"An' what's ya gonna name yer gun now that you're acquainted with her good shootin'?" asked Hawkins. "I named my piece 'Little Lightnin'."

"Um. . .How about 'Pearl,' after my mother?" answered Will.

"Pearl?" scoffed Jack. "What kinda handle is that fer the fine piece o' workmanship you're holdin' in yer hand?"

"I wish Mum was holding me just as tight. I plan to love this rifle like she loves me. How about you, Mac? What do you call your piece?"

"Hoot mon! Us MacDonalds aren't given to such sentimental drivel. The hard life of the Highlands cured us of that. I remember goin' a hunting with Father and gettin' lost in the fog. We had to spend the night on a lonely crag, so I lays down and gathers up some snow to rest me head on. I had just about fallen asleep, shivering as I was, when Father gives me a good kick. 'Are ye getting soft, laddie,' he snarled, 'usin' that snow fer a pillow?'"

"We best go inside, you grumpy old Scot," chortled Lightnin'. "Don't ya feel that sleet thumpin' ya on the head? We got so busy with our shootin', we plum fergot the nasty weather that keeps doggin' us."

# CHAPTER SIX: WINTER CAMP

Lightnin', Mac, and Will remained at Frazer's trading post for three more days, hoping the weather would break. Even though the sleet still fell on Thursday, they reluctantly threw on their coats and trudged off to the north along the Allegheny River trail. Will was now dressed as the others in buckskins. They all wore new heavy wool socks and three pairs of moccasins to keep their feet in good shape for the long hike back to their hunting grounds.

They continued along the trail for many days until they reached the splintered tree near their supply cache. When they arrived, they found the tracks of many Ottawas and an open pit yawning from the soggy earth.

"Thieving skunks!" growled Mac. "How could they have found what we hid so carefully?"

"Only takes one stray footprint we didn't brush away," muttered Lightnin'. "Them tracks look fresh. There must be thirty-some braves in their party. Let's streak it!"

The woodsmen scrambled up a deer path that bisected the main route. They rushed into the thick woods and ran for a full mile. There, Hawkins veered onto an even fainter trail that took them to a roaring freshet tumbling down a mountainside in a series of noisy, little waterfalls. After splashing across the stream, they climbed over a jumble of rocks where they'd leave no trail on the bare granite. Then, they slipped carefully through a laurel thicket, making sure not to break any telltale branches that could be seen by would-be pursuers.

When the mountain men cleared the laurel, they zigzagged back to the south and waded through the icy water of another stream for a half-mile. As they splashed wearily along, Will whispered, "Surely the Ottawas can't follow us now. How many more tricks do we have to use to keep them from finding our trail?"

"Can't be too careful," muttered Hawkins. "There was too many o' them scalp hunters to fight, so we gotta make sure they don't find us— ever."

Panting heavily, the trappers finally reached a path only Mac and Jack had trod. This they followed for five more miles until they reached a rude hut huddled in a glen. The hut was constructed Indian-style of logs and elm bark.

"Welcome home, laddie," said MacDonald, gesturing toward the cabin. "Here's where Jack and me wintered last year. It ain't much, but it keeps the snow off our noggins."

Will peered through an open doorway into the structure and found it barely large enough for the three of them to squeeze into. Sleeping benches, covered with bearskin blankets, were built into the sidewalls. A thicker bearskin served as a rug on the dirt floor. A few tools hung from pegs on the back wall, while beaver traps and long strings of dried corn hung from the rafters.

When a disappointed look passed over the lad's face, Lightnin' murmured, "Mac an' me built her small to make it harder fer enemies to find. She's mighty snug with a fire built near the door there."

"Aye, ye'll like her just fine, Will, once you're settled in," assured MacDonald. "There's no use buildin' a permanent cabin. We're just trappin' beaver here, not farmin' or startin' a settlement like the English want to do."

"Speakin' o' beaver," chortled Jack, "why don't we grab our five traps an' head over yonder to the next valley? It ain't more 'n' a quarter mile. Whole dang cities o' the tree gnawers live there."

"Why do you have so few traps?" asked Cutler.

"So few?" gasped Lightnin'. "Why we's lucky to have any with as scarce as they is. These was made fer us by an old blacksmith. The ones from England ain't available at all in these parts."

"Aye, most trappers use deadfalls an' snares to catch their beaver," muttered Alexander, "so we need to count our blessings."

The woodsmen gathered their gear and then tramped up a steep incline to the top of a hemlock-choked ridge. Skating down the other side, they emerged on the banks of a broad, winding creek. They hadn't crept more than fifty yards upstream before they came to a well-tended dam made of sticks, rocks, and mud. Scattered about the pond behind it were several huge beaver lodges constructed of more jagged branches. Everywhere were beaver sign, too, including fresh tree cuttings and burrows in the creek bank.

Cutler exchanged grins with his mentors and then cried, "Boy, there must be enough plews in this dam alone to pay for my rifle. How do we get started?"

"Wall now, Will, the first thing we do is set our trap by steppin' on the springs jess long

enough to hook one jaw beneath the back o' the pan."

"What's the pan?"

"It's the flat iron piece the beaver steps on to trigger the jaws," answered Mac.

"Oh, I see. Where do we put the trap once it's set?"

"I was just gettin' to that," Jack said, wading into the pond.

"Boy, that water looks cold!" exclaimed Will. "Why not just put the trap on the bank next to a beaver hole?"

"'Cause the beaver'd smell my scent before he sprung it. By puttin' it in the shallows, my stink gets washed off."

"But how will we know where the trap is hidden if it's underwater?"

"Well, laddie, Jack will drive in a pole next to it. Over the pole, he'll slide the chain attached to our trap. The chain will let the beaver reach deep water once he's caught. There, he'll drown before he can chew his leg off an' get away."

"I feel kind of bad for the beaver when you explain it like that," sighed Cutler.

"It's either him or us who survives," grunted Alexander. "This isn't any crueler than a farmer slaughterin' sheep or cattle."

"But how do we attract the beaver to the trap?" wondered Will. "Or does he find it all by himself?"

"That's where the medicine comes in," cackled Hawkins.

"Medicine?"

"That's what we call our bait," said Mac-Donald, uncorking a wooden bottle he carried on a thong dangling from his belt. "We dab a little on a branch that we stick in the lake above the trap. The medicine must be above the water so the beaver can get a good whiff."

"What's the bait made of?" Will asked. "It must be mighty strong to get him to swim way down here."

"It comes from the glands at the base of a beaver's tail," continued Alex. "The glands make a scent that he uses to mark his territory. We put the smell of a strange beaver in the other fellow's pond, an' it drives him bleedin' crazy. He has to come investigate once he gets a sniff. To stretch up an' smell the medicine, he puts his foot on the creek bottom an' pushes up. That's when he steps on the pan an' the jaws snap shut on his leg. Then, we got 'im!"

"That's enough talk, fellas," chided Hawkins. "Stop dawdlin'. We got traps to set."

"I hate working with me stomach rumblin'," countered Mac. "Shouldn't we have a trout dinner first?"

"Wagh!" yelped Jack. "Why didn't I think o' that?"

Lightnin' fetched a hand line made of dried milkweed stalks out his possibles bag. On the end of his line he tied a skewer. The skewer was made of bone and sharpened on both ends. The line was attached in a groove carved in the middle of the crude fish hook.

Hawkins furiously uprooted rocks along the creek until he found a fat white worm to thread on the skewer. Then, he crept off downstream to where a swift run disappeared beneath an undercut bank. He dropped his line into the water and let the current catch it. The worm barely disappeared before he was fast to a coal black fish that thrashed and yanked and fought with relentless vigor. Finally, Jack flipped the squirming trout onto the bank and pounced on it before it could flop back into the water. With a wide grin, he held up a nine inch brookie that seemed much larger while he fought it.

Mac baited his own hook and was soon hauling one trout after another from the deep pool below the beaver dam until he had caught seven fat fish for supper. Handing his fishing line to Will, he said, "Now, it's your turn, laddie. This is the most fun I've had since the day I stepped foot in the New World!"

Cutler made several clumsy underhand flips before finally hurling the line into the center of the pool. The worm swirled in the foaming current when a trout nailed the bait and charged off for its underwater lair. Will yanked so hard on the line that he pulled the skewer from the fish's mouth. The line flew back to wind itself endlessly around the surprised fisherman's arms and neck.

With a curse he heard used by one of Washington's woodsmen, the lad untangled himself and then rebaited the hook. Moving to the base of the dam, he hurled his line into the bubbling spume. He was immediately greeted by a sharp tug that nearly yanked the line from his hands. Shouting with surprise, Cutler scrambled down the bank to follow the trout's downstream run. The fish fought and splashed and shook its black head until Will finally worked it up on a gravel beach where Mac waited to collar it.

"Whoa!" cried Alexander, holding up the fourteen inch beauty. "Look at the red spots on this fellow. He's a meal in himself, he is. Congratulations, laddie."

"'Course, we ain't always gonna eat this fine," said Lightnin' as he built a fire to cook their fish. "Will, do ya know what else is in the woods to eat when there ain't meat?"

"Only those cattails we had awhile back. When I was with the Ottawas, I only ate what they grew or hunted down."

"Then, you was lucky," continued Hawkins. "Sometimes us boys has had to chaw milkweed shoots an' the tops o' stingin' nettles."

"Aye, an' bread can be made from dried clover heads," said Mac. "Dandelions aren't bad when boiled."

"When things got really tough, we biled lichen or et the bark o' pine an' willows," croaked Lightnin', making a sour face.

"Then, no wonder you and Alex are so tough," snickered Will. "I'll bet if the Indians ever try takin' your topknots, they'll break their knives instead."

# CHAPTER SEVEN: MAC'S STORY

"Wagh!  Look at the beaver we caught," yipped Jack when he and his partners returned to the pond the next day.

"We've got a fat little beastie in every trap!" exclaimed Alexander.  "We best go to a different pond this mornin'.  We don't want to clean this one out."

"But where will we find another dam this good?" asked Cutler.

"Just 'round the bend," chortled Lightnin'. "This valley is beaver heaven.  We's the only men ever been in these parts, I reckon.  If we's smart about it, we kin spend five more winters here."

"Unless someone else finds out where we trap," mumbled Will.

"Why do ya think we cut through all the rocks an' laurel returnin' to our camp?" asked Jack.

"So na other man could follow," assured MacDonald.

The woodsmen hadn't tramped upstream more than a half-mile before they discovered another beaver colony with even more lodges than the one where they'd been so successful.  This time they had Will set the long spring traps while they coached him.  By the time the lad had finished, he was nearly as skilled as his teachers at every phase of the procedure.

When the trappers returned to their hut, a dim lemon sun peeked through the winter clouds. It was succeeded in an instant by a misty rain and then light flurries. The men's breaths hung in the air as they puffed down the slope to their camp and huddled around the coals still glowing in the fire pit. Alexander added some kindling, and they soon had a fine fire to warm them.

"Now, it's time for a real treat," enthused Lightnin', pulling three beavers from his trapper's pack. Flopping the rodents on the ground, he cut off their flat tails and roasted them over the fire. When they were done to perfection, he handed one to Will.

"This tastes bad," gulped Cutler, after taking a bite from the tail. "Why, it's nothing but fat."

"Then, you ain't et the strips o' meat down the sides o' the tail bone," bristled Jack. "There's nothin' sweeter on God's green earth."

"Hey, I think it's time we teach the boy here how to skin beaver," said Mac as he devoured the other tail.

"Reckon so," answered Hawkins. "Let me fetch one o' the rascals, an' we'll start. Now, watch careful, Will, 'cause we won't get full price fer a plew if it ain't fleshed out proper."

Jack picked up a fat rodent and cut around its legs. Then, he started at the beaver's chin and cut its fur down the middle to the tail. After that, he peeled the hide over the legs and ended up with a round, soft pelt that he gave to Will to inspect.

Rising from the fire, Hawkins disappeared inside their hut and returned with a willow hoop. He stretched the plew on the hoop and began removing all the muscle tissue and fat from the back side of the skin. "Gettin' off all this tallow is the most important part," he grunted as he carefully sliced it with his knife. "If ya cut through the fur, it won't be worth a pinch o' sour owl manure. 'Least that's what Bob Winslow'd say."

When MacDonald picked up a second beaver to repeat the skinning process for Cutler, the boy asked Alexander, "How did you get into the fur business, Mac?  Didn't you like living in Scotland?"

"I did until the bleedin' English beat Bonnie Prince Charlie at Culloden.  The Prince was tryin' to restore the House of Stuart to the throne that's still held by that clootie, King George."

"Was Culloden a battle?"

"Aye, and what a battle it be, laddie!  I was but seventeen when I followed me clansmen onto Drummossie Moor."

"That's only a year older than me," whistled Will.  "What was it like to be a soldier?"

"Bloody frightenin'. We had to stand in the open while English cannon raked us with fire from across the marsh.  Not many a Scot was hit, but hearin' the shriek of those shells was enough to make a brave man tremble.  Standin' in line where the enemy can maul ya is not my idea o' fightin'.  The Indian notion o' 'one man, one tree' be far better for keepin' a soldier's limbs where they belong."

"That must o' been bad," observed Hawkins, "'cause I ain't ever seen you afraid o' nothin', Mac."

"Aye, but that weren't the worst of it.  The boggy ground made the Scottish charge nigh unto impossible."

"What's a Scottish charge?" asked Will, edging closer so not to miss a word.

"That's when we rouse our ire and hit the enemy on the run, whirlin' our swords and axes

Reenactor, John Stengel, poses as a Scottish soldier as he may have looked at the Battle of Culloden.

like the Ottawas do here. We smash 'em so hard, their line buckles--every time."

"But not at Culloden?"

"Na, 'cause us MacDonalds refused to join in. We was mad at Prince Charlie for denyin' us our usual place o' honor on the right flank. Bein' on the left made even Father irate."

"What's the difference where you fought, as long as ya got a crack at the Government?" asked Jack.

"Scottish pride is the curse o' me clan, but it wasn't why we lost. The English had more muskets. Their fire be too brutal to bear. Then, the traitorous Campbells got around our flank. That forced our retreat. As we left the field, we heard that butcher, Cumberland, order our wounded shot like curs. Those holed up in a sheep hut were burned alive. They included me own father, who'd been shot through both ankles. I'll never forgive them that!"

Mac's voice trailed off, and a single tear trickled down his ruddy cheek. A moment later he cried, "After the battle the Government rounded up prisoners. Killed them in cold blood. Soon, they passed laws forbiddin' kilt and tartan. They killed the clansmen. Then the clan. That's when I come to America."

"How did you get here?" asked Will, giving Alex a sympathetic pat on the shoulder.

"An agent came round me village an' asked who wished to emigrate to America. With most o' me family gone, I jumped at the chance. I had enough money for the passage, but the ship captain wouldn't take it when I boarded his vessel. He said we'd pay when we got to Philadelphia."

"That happened to Father and me, too," remembered Will. "Our ship was so full of thieves, we took turns staying awake so no one could steal our fare."

"I not be that lucky," muttered Mac. "Some sailors invited me to have a drink with them. They kept fillin' me tankard with rum until I passed out from it. When a thumpin' headache brought me to, me pounds was gone. I went straight to the captain, I did, an' pointed out the rascals who stole from me. His lordship wouldn't believe 'a lyin' Scot,' so I thrashed the varlets on me own. Then, it was me who got ten lashes from the cat-o'-nine-tails for strikin' royal navy men. So much for the King's justice."

"That's mighty harsh," growled Lightnin'. "An' yet the English call Indians savages."

"Oh, but things got even worse when we reached America," groaned Mac. "The captain anchored in the harbor o' Philadelphia, so none o' us Scots could leave the ship. Those o' us who lost our money was made indentured servants to the rich swine who paid our passage. One husband an' wife had twins durin' our voyage. 'Why should we pay for the bairns,' they asked, 'when they weren't alive when we boarded?' It didn't matter. Their master added ten years to their servitude. There's plenty of reasons to hate the English!"

"Who did you work for?" inquired Will.

"A retired redcoat captain is who. He may have left the army, but the army didn't leave him. Aye, life with that bleedin' man was an endless string o' orders. An' anything that shat, I cleaned up after. If I didn't move fast enough for his liking, he smacked me with his cane, he did. Finally, one night I busted that cane over his

Not all woodsmen of the 1750's wore buckskins. Like many trappers, John Stengel is dressed in a linen smock. He is carrying a Brown Bess smoothbore musket used by the British army.

square head. Grabbin' his old Brown Bess, I run out the door an' headed for the wilderness. To avoid the constables, I ended up out Susquehanna way. I'd have starved to death, too, if Jack hadn't taken me under his wing. For that, I be ever thankful."

"Hey, weren't nothin'," replied Hawkins with a self-conscious grin. "When I seen how ill-fitted you be, I had to help. Why, you was stompin' through the snow with no coat an' the most forlorn look planted on that face o' yers. I'd do the same fer any lost soul. An' we've had our adventures. An' close scrapes, too. Did I ever tell you boys 'bout the first time I run into them Ottawas? That was before you an' me trapped together, Mac."

"Many times," replied the Scot with a roll of his eyes, "but ye might tell the lad here."

"Wall, it all happened back in '50, or mebbe '51. I had killed a big gobbler in them Ottawas' huntin' grounds, an' they didn't take kindly to it no how. They ketched me in the middle o' guttin' that turkey an' chased me fer miles. I exchanged shots with 'em 'til I run out o' powder, too. Then, I hid my rifle an' lit out fer the river like a buck spooked by mountain lions. Only problem was, I didn't know the woods I was streakin' through."

"Where did you end up, then?" asked Will, his eyes wide with anticipation.

"I had them red men 'bout outrun when I comes to this meadow. There, I raced even faster 'til I sees the grass kinda end like. I skidded to a stop just afore pitchin' over a forty-foot cliff."

"Wasn't that cliff thirty feet?" asked Mac with a mischievous smile. "I swear it be the last time ye told this tale."

"Thirty feet, forty feet, what's the diff'rence? All I know is that I was now surrounded by sixty howlin' Indians, each one thirstin' fer my topknot. They started creepin' in on three sides 'til one brave rushed to whack me with his hatchet. I dodged just in time, stuck him with my knife, an' grabbed the ax as he fell dead. Then, I slashed with the hatchet to keep them others at bay."

"Boy, you really were in a fix!" gasped Will.

"I figgered I was a gone beaver, fer sure. In my mind I could see them Ottawas stickin' hot splinters in my flesh 'til I glances below an' spies a tall dead oak to climb down. There was only one problem. . ."

"What was that?" croaked Cutler, hugging himself to quell his goose bumps.

"The biggest bar I ever seen had climbed up that oak to get honey. The Indians was just 'bout breathin' on me by then, so I jumps on the bar's back. He give out a mighty roar but couldn't shake me off without fallin' hisself. That got 'im so riled he fergot all 'bout that honey an' starts down the tree with me clingin' to his back for all I was worth. The air was thick with arrows, too, as them Ottawas was raisin' a mighty commotion above an' firing their bows faster 'n' lightnin'."

"Not as fast as you, though," chuckled Mac.

"No, I was way ahead o' all them rascals, 'cause I let go o' that bar an' hit the ground runnin'. Why, I run so fast even them arrows wasn't gonna ketch me. An' that's the God honest truth!"

"Aye, even if it be twenty red men that chased ye the last time," teased Alexander.

# CHAPTER EIGHT:
## AN AMBUSH GONE AWRY

Jack Hawkins crept along the forest floor with Alexander and Will close at his heels. Huge hemlocks dwarfed the hunters and immersed them in thick shadow. The wind whipped wildly, rocking the tree boughs and freezing the men's faces. A thick snow showered from the obscure December sky, cutting visibility even further.

Jack stopped every few steps as his sharp eyes searched for the furtive movement of an elusive four-legged quarry. Often, he sniffed the air for the scent of concealed deer that he would recognize from fifty yards. He was certain that most herds would be bedded down in such horrible conditions.

Noiselessly, the three hunters slunk forward until they reached a recognized trail. Here, they moved even slower, knowing from the fresh hoof prints in the deepening snow that a doe and two yearlings were just ahead. Jack's stomach growled from hunger, and he felt a rush of excitement at the fresh deer sign.

Hawkins' skin prickled as an even stronger sensation crept into his brain. It was the warning of an enemy, unseen yet imminent. He raised his hand to alert his partners and then silently scanned the woods ahead. Although he saw nothing, he cocked his long rifle and raised it to his shoulder. Now, he stopped after every step to sniff the air and listen for the snapping of twigs or the crunch of an errant footfall. All he heard was MacDonald and Cutler cocking their pieces, as well.

Jack was so intent upon sniffing out an ambush that he didn't notice a gnarled woodsman appear like a ghost from the swirling snow behind them. Undetected, the old trapper followed the men for several minutes with a mischievous grin shining in his white, chest-length beard. Finally, the fellow sniggered, "Don't you boys know them scalp thieves don't always hit ya from the front?"

"Why, Bearbite Bob Winslow, you old coot," yelped Jack, just about dropping his rifle, "you jess scared me out o' ten years o' my life!"

"Aye," croaked Alexander, "an' ye scared me so bad, me mother screamed in Scotland."

"If I'da been Ottawas, you'd be dead now. You still got a lot to learn 'bout watchin' yer topknot."

"A-A-And that's one lesson I'll never f-f-forget," stuttered Will.

"What's you boys doin' out on a day not fit fer a wolf pack?" asked Bob.

"We was on the trail o' three deer 'til you come along," grumbled Hawkins.

"Ah, fergit them," urged the old trapper.

"But we haven't eaten in three days," muttered Mac.

"Then chaw on this," chortled Winslow, digging some fresh jerky from his possibles bag. "How'd ya do trappin' this fall?"

"Fair to middlin'," answered Jack evasively. "How 'bout you?"

"I got my share!" cackled Bearbite.

"You always do."

"Now, that the beaver ponds is froze over, why don't you join me on a real hunt? Where I'm goin' there's elk an' even a buffalo er two."

"Where's that?" asked Will, with a wide grin.

"Across the river. Over Logstown way."

"But there's three Indian villages in them parts," objected Jack. "How can there be much game left over yonder?"

"Come along fer a ride in my new canoe, an' I'll shows ya."

"You must be gettin' old if ya need a canoe to cross the Allegheny," kidded Hawkins. "Last year you'd have swum fer it."

"An' you'da jumped across in one bound, or so you's always braggin'."

"Alright, we'll go," sighed MacDonald. "We sure haven't found enough game over here to feed us."

With Bob leading the way, the other trappers followed him down the deer path to a well-traveled trail. This they took to the west, bowing into the driving snow. When they reached the banks of the cold Allegheny, the old trapper skated onto a beach that he followed upriver to a laurel thicket protruding from the neighboring woods.

Hidden in the laurel was a long, elm bark canoe that one man would have difficulty handling. When Jack spied the craft, he exclaimed, "Wagh! That looks like one of them big rascals the Frenchies is always paddlin'. How'd you come by it, anyhow, Bearbite?"

"Let's jess say it come loose from its moorin' ropes. I couldn't let it crush itself in the rapids. 'T wouldn't be neighborly. If I ever run into its owners, I reckon they'll give me a big, fat reward."

"Aye!" laughed Alexander. "An' it'll probably be in powder an' balls fired from the end o' their muskets."

"Wall, we best not stand here prattlin' like a bunch o' old fishwives," chided Winslow, glancing nervously upriver. "Let's get after them elk I was tellin' ya 'bout."

Bob and Jack yanked the canoe from its place of concealment and carried it to the beach. After pushing its bow into the water, Bearbite, Will, and Lightnin' climbed inside and snatched up paddles. Mac shoved them into the river and leaped into the stern all in the same motion. In an instant they were rushing with the current through a long chute of rapids. Pelted by a blizzard wind, they angled toward the far bank. They whisked along listening to the snow hiss as it hit the water.

It only took ten minutes to reach the far bank. Immediately, they sprang from their craft and dragged it into the thick hemlock with Bob urging them on. After covering the canoe with dead branches, Bearbite hustled them into the woods until they were safely out of view of the river.

The hunters fanned out in a line a few yards apart and began looking for signs of elk, deer, or buffalo. They hadn't gone more than a couple miles when they heard a shot echo from the trees ahead. Diving for cover, they cocked their long rifles and lay quivering with cold and anticipation. When no other shots rang out, Jack hissed, "Can't be them canoe owners you seemed so anxious to shed, Bearbite, er that gun woulda been fired behind us. Let's put the creeps on him who shot it."

"Probably jess another hunter," grunted Bob. "I told ya there's a mess o' game here."

"Then, mebbe he needs help guttin' his kill. We could get some fresh liver to gnaw on if we lend a hand," Hawkins said, licking his lips.

"Is it smart to betray our position?" asked Mac, giving Winslow a rueful look. "What if it is the Frenchies out a lookin' for a thief?"

"Couldn't we just c-c-cut around them?" stammered Will.

"If all o' you is scared, I reckon I'll go myself," retorted Jack.

"Now, hold on thar!" bristled Bob. "Who said we's scared? Come on, boys, let's find out who burned powder."

Jack and the others crawled silently to their feet and inched along peering through the undergrowth. They again moved single file with the curious Hawkins leading the way. When they reached the edge of a little clearing, Lightnin' signaled for them to stop. Just ahead were two white men wrestling an Indian to the ground. The brave thrashed and kicked while the others tried binding him with a stout rope.

When the Indian almost squirmed free, Jack burst from the brush and threatened the muscular savage with his gun. Looking into the red man's fierce face, he gasped, "Bold Wolf, you rascal! What mischief you causin' this time?"

"Tryin' to kill Washington here!" exclaimed one of the tall travelers who struggled to fasten Bold Wolf's bonds.

"Christopher Gist? Major Washington? What's you fellas doin' out here in the woods all by yer lonesome?"

"The major insisted we strike off 'cross this wilderness to reach Virginia quicker," replied Gist ruefully. "Said the others was slowin' us up. Is that you, Bearbite, skulkin' back in them bushes? How ya doin'?"

"Fine as frog's fur," chuckled Bob as he, Will, and Alexander stepped into the clearing brandishing their guns. "What's goin' on here?"

"We met this savage back in Murderin' Town, an' he offered to guide us. Insisted, actually," puffed Christopher as he tied another knot to secure Bold Wolf's bonds.

"Ain't that a 'propriate place to meet this devil," interjected Bearbite. "But go on."

"Like I was sayin'," continued Gist, "he said he knew a shortcut to the Forks of the Ohio. I thought I saw this rascal in Venango, but he called me by my Indian name an' come on real friendly like."

"Yes, like the sneaking scalp thief he is!" snarled Will, snatching his hatchet from his belt. "He killed my father. Now, it's my turn!"

George Washington leaped up and stepped between Cutler and Bold Wolf. "No, stop!" barked the major. "Killing this man can't bring your father back. You don't want his blood on your hands."

"But didn't he want your blood?" shrieked Will.

"The major's right, laddie," said Mac, grabbing the boy by the shoulders to restrain him. "We still haven't heard what Bold Wolf did, and you're already convictin' him. To me, it smacks of the same justice Butcher Cumberland used in the Highlands."

"Yes, Gist, tell us what this devil's done," said Jack, "an' we won't interrupt ya again."

"Wall now, this heathen led us some ten mile to the south toward the Forks. By then, we was mighty weary, so George wants to camp. Then, the Wolf here says we must keep goin', an' if the major's tired, he'll carry his gun fer him. When George refuses, he urges us to hurry 'cause there's some Ottawas in the woods who's after our scalps."

"He should know!" shrieked Will, struggling to free himself from Mac's grasp. "He's their chief!"

"Calm down thar, boy," commanded Christopher. "You want every warrior in the area down on us? Do ya want to hear my story, or not?"

"Go on! Go on!" urged Hawkins. "Otherwise, I'm gonna bust."

"Yes, jess like my wheezin' lungs when our deceitful friend here starts leadin' us north. When George asks where we's goin', Wolf says he's got a cabin two whoops away where we'll be safe. Then, he has us stomp two more mile, still away from the Forks. That's when the major put his foot down. He tells our guide we's gonna camp at the next place we comes to water. Soon after, we enters this clearin', and this rascal whirls an' shoots. Before he can ram home another ball, we jumps him. That's when you come along."

"How far away was he when he shot at you?" croaked Cutler.

"Fifteen paces," answered Gist.

"Good thing he had a trade rifle, or you'd be a gone beaver!" exclaimed Bob. "Couldn't hit a bear in the be-hind with one o' them guns."

"Well, what do ya want to do, Major?" asked Lightnin'. "Us boys'll be glad to guide you. We know every flea on the squirrels' backs in these parts."

"No, just point the way," replied Washington. "If there really are hostiles after us, we'll have a better chance of shaking them if Christopher and I go on alone."

"What about Bold Wolf?" growled Will, again struggling to free himself from Mac.

"Let him go," said the major.

"What?" gasped Cutler.

"I'll not have any man killed in cold blood while I'm in command. Cut him loose, Gist."

"Yes, sir," grunted Christopher with a reluctant scowl. "But I'll jess foller him into the woods to make sure he goes."

After Gist sliced through his bonds, Bold Wolf gave each of his captors a cold stare as if to fix their faces in his mind. In the next instant, he leaped into the brush and disappeared like an evil apparition. Gist cocked his rifle and stepped into the undergrowth to follow. After a few minutes, he returned and said, "That rapscallion ain't gonna bother us no more. He done fled this here country like a bobcat after a fast rabbit."

"Or went to find his band of Ottawas," suggested Washington. "Let's go, Christopher, while there's still light to find the Allegheny."

"Jess foller our tracks," instructed Bearbite, "an' you'll come right to her."

"Thanks for all your help," replied the major, shaking hands with Bob and Jack before hurrying off into the woods. "Good luck to you, men."

"Now, what are we going to do?" asked Mac, finally releasing Will from his grasp.

"Go to Logstown where them Ottawas can't harm us," cackled Winslow. "No use sleepin' in the cold snow, anyhow, when we kin have a fine squaw to drive the chill from our bones."

"But what 'bout all them elk and buffalo, we was supposed to find in these here parts?" grumbled Lightnin'. "Or was that jess a trick to get us to stomp all this way? Come on, fess up, Bearbite."

"I reckon you wouldn'ta come with me if there weren't game involved," snickered the old trapper. "But I'd jess as soon skin a squaw as a tough old buffalo any day o' the week."

"Ain't you kinda old fer them type o' urges?" asked Jack.

"The only time I'll be that old is when some hos-tile hangs my scalp on his lodge pole," cackled Bob with a sly wink.

"Or a jealous husband," needled Alex.

"Wagh, Mac! You're almost as serious as that Washington feller. I'm sure glad he ain't goin' ta Logstown with us 'cause he ain't no fun."

"Na, but he has a sense of honor," replied MacDonald. "He's one officer I wouldn't mind followin' if there be a war."

"Ya sure know who's in charge when the major's around," added Jack. "I'd hate bein' on his bad side."

"The only thing I'd hate is bein' caught by them Ottawas before we go a squawin'," groused Bearbite. "Let's git, while the gittin's good!"

# CHAPTER NINE: LOGSTOWN

Bearbite Bob gave a whoop and pointed to the Indian village rising from the banks of the Ohio River ahead. "Look, fellers, it's Logstown," he bellowed.

"Yes, we know," groaned Lightnin', "where you're gonna skin a squaw. What attracts 'em to an old coot like you, anyhow?"

"Indian gals love my beard. It tickles 'em like no clean-shaved red man can. Jess watch me work!"

The trappers came out of the woods onto snowy streets that wove helter-skelter through a maze of wigwams, log huts, and longhouses. Merchant tents took up the spaces in between where white men speaking many tongues bartered with the natives. Smoke rising from chimneys and smoke holes gave the town a cozy appearance as flurries floated from the dark sky.

When the woodsmen started up the nearest thoroughfare, Bob spied a comely Indian lass sweeping snow from the entrance of her wigwam. Strolling up to her, he doffed his coonskin cap and spoke flatteringly in Shawnee. His words had barely left Bearbite's lips when the maiden sidled around him and applied her broom vigorously to the backside of his pants. She cursed his name and continued to beat him until Winslow sought refuge among his snickering friends.

Before Jack could deride Bearbite, the old trapper spotted another less attractive Indian emerging from her log hut. With a winning smile, he sauntered over to the woman and cooed in Wyandot until a shocked look passed over her face. The squaw unleashed a keening wail and smacked Bob with her hard fists. When he raised his arms to fend her off, she added two telling kicks to speed him back to his roaring pals.

Still not to be denied, Bearbite approached a more middle-aged squaw who came toward them up the street carrying a blanket she had bought from one of the French merchants. Bob whispered to her in the Delaware language and pointed suggestively to her blanket. Spewing a guttural mix of rage and loathing, she drew a knife and lunged at Bearbite's gut. Dodging with an agility that belied his age, the woodsman just missed being gored. To escape her wrath, Winslow dove behind a group of chuckling peddlers until the Delaware woman shook her head in disgust and disappeared up the street.

With a sheepish grin, Bob rejoined his friends. While the crestfallen, old trapper inspected the tops of his moccasins, Hawkins jeered, "If that's how ya hook up with a squaw, I'll stick ta huntin' anytime."

"Aye," snickered Mac. "I'd rather be run down by stampedin' buffalo than trifle with those grrrls."

"How come there's women of so many tribes in Logstown, anyway?" asked Will with a smirk.

"'Cause it's the most important village in these parts," replied MacDonald, stifling another chuckle. "It's a trading center an' the place where the Half-King, Tanacharison, holds council. He's the Iroquois leader who rules here. All the other tribes were conquered by the Iroquois an' are scared to death o' them."

Reenactors, Jerry Roberts and James Selander, pose as merchants like those who dealt with the Indians at Logstown.

"Is that because they're cannibals?" croaked Cutler. "That's the rumor I heard while living with the Ottawas."

"Wouldn't know fer sure," chuckled Jack. "But in this town, I'd check the bones in my stew before I et any of it."

"Speakin' o' the Iroquois, there's their part o' town jess ahead," said Bearbite, a glimmer of hope glinting in his eyes. "Come on. I know all the gals there."

"I shore hope none of 'em's carryin' a hatchet," chortled Jack.

The trappers meandered up the street until they arrived at the first longhouse in an extended row. The building was over one hundred feet in length and twenty feet wide. Made of a wooden frame, it towered twenty feet above them and was covered with elm bark. Jack counted six smoke holes that were used by the families living inside. He remembered that each longhouse provided shelter for a village's entire Iroquois clan. From the eight different buildings, he knew that these were Senecas because this tribe was divided into the Bear, Wolf, Turtle, Snipe, Deer, Beaver, Heron, and Hawk clans.

While Lightnin' was inspecting the Iroquois' dwelling, Bob spied a heavy-set squaw squatting on an outside bench repairing fishing spears. Immediately, he shouted, "Wagh! Bear Woman. It's your Bear Man come back to ya."

The woman's head swiveled around on her thick neck, and she let out a screech that sent Jack, Will, and Mac diving to the ground to escape flying projectiles. Instead, the squaw dropped her spears in the snow and came bounding across the street to catch Bearbite in a powerful embrace. With a celebratory cackle, he returned her hug and then rubbed his whiskers down her cheeks and neck. She giggled with childlike joy, grabbed him by the beard, and led him toward the Bear clan longhouse.

Bob whispered to Bear Woman in Iroquois and then motioned for his friends to follow them inside her home. "Come on," he shouted, "I got you boys invited fer dinner."

"I just hope we're not one of the courses," gulped Will.

"Don't worry, boy," joshed Lightnin'. "I hear them Senecas ain't fond o' white meat."

The trappers cautiously approached the door leading into the longhouse and peered inside. Within the dim interior were six central hearths glowing with coals to provide warmth for the family compartments. Sleeping benches lined the walls, and tools, cornstalk dolls, extra moccasins, and countless other personal items stuck out from beneath them. Above the benches hung storage racks and strings of dried corn and squash. Every inch of space was put to functional use by the Bear clan.

Bear Woman led her guests to the second hearth and began preparing them a hot meal. Into wooden bowls she dipped some corn soup, which she passed to each man in turn. Then, she scooped some hominy made of dried corn and beans onto wooden plates. The trappers found both foods delicious and wolfed them down until satisfied grins wreathed their faces.

Will had just finished his hominy when he saw a lithe girl with dainty features enter the main entrance of the longhouse. She wore an overdress, skirt, and leggings all made of deer hide and heavily decorated with beadwork. Her hair was long but not as dark as the other

Iroquois maidens. Instead of the usual leather headband, she wore a tiara beaded with the Celestial Sky design.

The girl walked with such fluid motion that she seemed to float across the hide rugs covering the floor. When she drew even with Will, he gasped at her beauty, and a silly grin spread across his face. He waved at her vaguely and gurgled "Hello," but she moved on past without as much as acknowledging his existence.

Winslow was quick to note Will's infatuation. Clapping him on the back, Bob chortled, "So you loves squaws, too. But if ya wants ta keep yer topknot, ya best find one more common than the likes o' her."

"W-W-Who was that?" choked the lad, his eyes still following the wispy girl as she passed into another compartment.

"Bright Star is who! She's Dark Thunder's daughter. Her pa's the sachem of this here tribe an' would eat yer liver, roasted or not, if ya tries anything."

"What do you mean by 'tries anything'?" muttered Cutler, stiffening with anger. "A fellow marries a girl like that."

"Whoa, there!" exclaimed Hawkins. "You best be a mighty brave before you starts such talk. That's the only kind o' man Bright Star's ma will pick fer her."

"Pick for her?"

"Aye, laddie, don't ye know that Iroquois mothers arrange all the marriages?" Alex asked. "Why would ye be lookin' for a squaw, anyhow, when there's plenty o' fine civilized girls a comin' to the frontier?"

"She was civilized once," countered Cutler. "Didn't you see her blue eyes? Why, she'll be perfect for me, being we've both been captives."

"What was it like livin' with them Ottawas?" asked Jack.

"It was scary at first because I thought they were going to kill me during my adoption into the tribe. The day after they took me to their village, they started plucking out my hair like I was a turkey. Then, they drilled a hole in my nose and in both ears and fastened rings in them. Talk about torture! I thought I was a goner when they stripped off my clothes, painted me from head to foot, and took me to their chief. After he made a long speech, he gave me to three young girls who led me into the river, no doubt to drown me."

"Three young squaws, ya say?" cackled Bob. "What a way ta go!"

"Um, as I was sayin'," continued Will, clearing his throat, "these girls made signs for me to dive into the water. When I didn't do it, they forced me to, scrubbing and rubbing at me like mad. Finally, when I was clean, they took me to the council house where I was given gifts and new clothes. Then, a chief welcomed me into the tribe, and I had the same freedom as everyone else. If Bold Wolf hadn't lived in that village, I would have loved my new life."

"Don't speak that devil's name!" admonished Winslow, seeing how Bear Woman recoiled at the mention of it. "How do ya expect me to get any lovin' if you scares it all out o' my gal?"

"I'm sorry. I just wish the Iroquois had the wooing dance I saw at a Wyandot town. Then, we both could court our ladies."

"In the Highlands dancing was me only joy," sighed Mac. "How did the Indians do theirs?"

71

"Well, the boys and girls formed two lines facing each other. Then, they started singing 'ya ne no hoo, ya ne no hoo' over and over while one of them shook a rattle. The two lines moved for'ard until the dancers' heads touched. Until they moved back and formed again, they whispered in each others' ears without bein' overheard. That dance went on for hours."

"How many dances did you do?" asked Bob with a leering grin.

"None. No girls like Bright Star were there."

"You're mighty partic'lar fer a hoop maker's boy," chided Lightnin'.

"Is that so? Then, why aren't you rubbing your whiskers on some squaw's neck?"

"'Cause I'm married to the wind, is why. I'd die if I had to stay penned up in a longhouse with my wife's clan. That's what's expected if ya marries up with one of 'em."

"That don't sound so bad to me now that trappin' season's over," guffawed Bob. "Why don't you fellers git lost fer a while, so me an' Bear Woman kin git reacquainted?"

"Aye, we best be headed back to winter camp, anyhow," replied Mac. "We'll get soft stayin' here."

"Yes, the wind's a callin'!" exclaimed Hawkins. "Are ya comin', Will?"

"I guess so," mumbled Cutler, casting one last adoring glance at Bright Star, who was moving about her family's compartment readying her parents' supper. "I got a lot to prove before I come to Logstown again."

# CHAPTER TEN: THE FRENCH INVASION

The next spring Jack, Mac, and Will bundled up their beaver plews and started out for Frazer's to trade for another year's supplies. As they left their hut in the little glen, Hawkins said, "We done mighty fine trappin' ag'in. If I was a religious fella, I'd pray to God an' thank 'im fer all He provided."

"That's what the Ottawas did," replied Will. "They even thanked the Great Spirit for every deer they killed."

"Then, I'll say a silent prayer for us," offered Mac, "while we be stompin' along."

The woodsmen took their time tramping the paths that led back to the Allegheny. They had lain around most of the winter swapping yarns and mending their clothes and tools and weren't in very good walking shape. They also moved slowly to enjoy the shrill song of the redwing blackbird and the joyous music provided by hundreds of creatures awakening from hibernation.

The trappers had just returned to the main trail that led south along the river when a beaver slapped its tail to warn them of danger. The men dove for cover in a laurel thicket and peered from hiding to witness an eye-popping spectacle. There before them floated a long string of canoes and bateaux filled with a huge army of French and Indians.

Mac gasped at the sight of the flat-bottomed boats that were pointed on the ends and propelled by four rowers and a pole man. Most of the bateaux were crammed to the gunwales with marines decked out in grayish-white justacorp coats and knee-length breeches. Still other boats hauled six-pound cannons and their gun crews dressed in dark blue. All the soldiers were armed with Charleville muskets and wore black tricorner hats and gaiters. MacDonald noted that they were well-provisioned, as well, with bulging fur knapsacks, linen haversacks, and gourd-shaped bottles, no doubt filled with rum.

All around the fleet of bateaux skimmed endless canoes manned by Indian warriors and French-Canadian irregulars wearing buckskins. Will grimaced and nudged Mac when he saw Bold Wolf in the stern of a canoe that passed just in front of them. "I'd shoot him in a minute," hissed the lad, "if there weren't so many of them."

"Aye, this army must be a thousand strong," croaked Alexander, "and sent to invade the land hereabout. If we'd had all these marines at Culloden instead of the Regiment Ecossais Royaux, we'd have carried off Bloody Cumberland's head on a pig pole."

"An' look at them cannon!" whispered Jack. "There must be fort buildin' planned, too."

"We best follow them, then," recommended MacDonald.

"Should we take our canoe?" asked Hawkins. "We hid it not far from here."

"Na, we don't want to overtake them an' get captured. We be better spies a peeking from the bushes."

The woodsmen remained in hiding for well over an hour watching the French invasion force stream by. Then, they waited awhile longer to make sure a canoe full of Indians wasn't lagging behind to guard the rear of the flotilla. When the river birds again took up their songs, the trappers crept from their places of concealment and stretched their knotted muscles. Strapping their heavy fur bundles on their backs, they stole off downriver, with their eyes peeled for the enemy.

The mountain men's deliberate pace limited them to only ten miles that day. When darkness fell, they scanned the sky for French campfires but saw nothing but a crescent moon rise above the treetops. Taking refuge beneath an undercut bank, they slept fitfully, listening to owls exchange hoots until the wee hours of the morning.

At the first glimmer of dawn, the men gobbled down some cold jerky they dug from their possibles bags and then crept cautiously down the trail. When they still hadn't encountered the French by noon, Lightnin' said, "Them boys must be travelin' night an' day."

"Aye, the river's so full o' melted snow, they needn't worry 'bout snags," answered Mac. "We might as well walk a little faster, or we'll never catch 'em. Should we cache our furs? That'd make the goin' a bit easier."

"No, we still need to trade fer supplies when we get to Frazer's."

"And I have to pay for my long rifle," reminded Will.

Shouldering their burdens, the woodsmen marched glumly along for several more days. When they neared the Forks of the Ohio, they heard the ringing of axes just ahead. Concealing their furs in the undergrowth, they crept on all fours to the edge of a new clear-cut. Peering through the brush, Lightnin' gave a low whistle and pointed toward a French work party hacking the branches from freshly felled oaks and hemlocks at the forest edge.

Will and Mac carefully parted the bushes and stared out at a landscape scarred by new construction. For a good quarter mile lay a desolate plain that had been stripped of all timber. Across this plain sweating soldiers hauled logs and dug a maze of ditches. Beyond the ditches rose a new fort from the confluence of the Allegheny and Monongahela that made the woodsmen gasp in wonder.

With a trained eye, MacDonald took note of the fort's main features. Along the banks of the two rivers workmen toiled to erect a stockade wall of round logs that Alex estimated to be twelve feet high. On the land side other soldiers were building a rampart of squared logs backfilled with dirt. Even more impressive were the bastions being raised on the four corners of the stronghold on which to place the eighteen cannons that now occupied the parade ground. The enclosure, when finished, would be 150 feet square and nearly impenetrable. Even the main entrance, which faced the east, was protected by a gate and a drawbridge.

"Why did the Frenchies clear so much land?" whispered Will. "That must be really hard work."

"To keep their fort out o' musket range," answered Jack.

"Aye, an' to have room for corn plantin' an' bark huts," added Alexander. "They don't want the Ottawas living inside the walls with 'em."

"I seen enough. How 'bout you, Mac?" gulped Lightnin'. "Let's hoof it!"

The woodsmen had just risen to their haunches when a French work party blundered into the forest lugging double-bladed axes. Staggering along like dazed bears, the exhausted men came within a few feet of Mac without seeing him. Finally, they stumbled toward the nearest tree and flopped on the ground to pant and groan.

Jack, Alex, and Will, meanwhile, sank back into the brush and lay flat. Hardly daring to breathe, they listened to the Frenchmen jabber in tired staccato and watched them pull frequently from their gourd bottles. Just before Lightnin' could signal his friends to rush the intruders blocking their escape, the fatigued soldiers curled up together at the base of an oak and fell asleep.

With the Frenchmen's snoring loud in their ears, the trappers rose from hiding and tiptoed off into the forest. Stopping only long enough to snag their fur bundles, Jack, Mac, and Will then rushed headlong down the trail leading to Frazer's trading post. They never stopped running until the log structure loomed out of the brush ahead. Charging around the end of the building, they found a ragtag group of Virginians gathered before Frazer's door talking in excited voices.

"Them Frenchies surprised us, they did," lamented a lanky ensign. "There was a thousand of them to forty of us boys. An' they had a battery of cannon pointed at us. What was we supposed to do, Lieutenant Frazer, but surrender?"

"You did the right thing, Ward," replied John. "What did you say that French captain's name was again?"

"Contrecoeur. He was the most polite feller I come across in all my born days. He even invited me to supper after I done handed over our half-built fort to him."

"It's a good thing he was in command," offered another Virginia militiaman, with a shiver. "You shoulda seen how them Indians of his was lookin' at us. We'da all been butchered if them devils had their way."

"An' that Frenchie let us take our tools, too," added a third man. "He was a real gent, he was."

"An' now that gent's a buildin' a huge fort where yours musta stood," blustered Lightnin', striding forward with Will and Mac to join in the conversation. "An' what are we gonna do about it?"

"Tell Washington," urged Frazer.

"That's already being taken care of," sighed Ensign Ward. "I sent a man to Redstone Creek with the news."

"Then, ye better send another runner," cried Mac, "an' tell the major how the fort is bein' laid out. I got it all in my head, if one o' you will write it down."

# CHAPTER ELEVEN: A TOUGH JOURNEY

"I have a proposition for you boys," said John Frazer as Will handed him a bundle of prime plews to pay for his long rifle.

"What's that, John?" asked MacDonald, piling a new skinning knife, several pigs of lead, and a horn of black powder on the trader's counter.

"I'm in a bit of a pickle, Mac. Henry Miller usually carries my furs to Will's Creek. Yestiddy, some fellas found 'im in the woods. His neck had been broke, but there weren't no explanation why. He hadn't fallen off a horse or cliff or nothin'. He was jess layin' along the trail deader 'n' grunt."

"Was Miller scalped?" croaked Alexander.

"No."

"Then, maybe the Frenchies got 'im," suggested Hawkins. "They already drove you out o' Venango, so I reckon they don't want ya operatin' in these parts neither."

"You're prob'ly right, Lightnin'. How 'bout you boys sellin' my furs fer me? I got horses you kin use, an' I'll give ya two Gin traps fresh from England an' all that Mac put on the counter fer yer trouble."

"Yes, let's help him!" exclaimed Will. "I sorta miss handling horses since Father was killed."

"An' those Gin traps are mighty valuable," Mac calculated. "How 'bout it, Lightnin'?"

"Why not. With the woods up yonder crawl-in' with Frenchies, Potawatomis, an' Ottawas, it'd be a might healthier down Fort Cumberland way."

Frazer led the trappers to his stables where three chestnut mares and a black gelding were quartered. The horses fidgeted and snorted as the visitors entered, and Alexander chuckled, "They must smell that bear grease ye smeared yourself with all winter, Jack. Why do ye do that?"

"Keeps my skin from splittin' open is why. Let's get these critters loaded an' head off down the trail. There's a storm brewin'. That's probably what's got 'em so nervous."

"Or the thoughts of carrying those heavy packs," muttered Cutler, pointing to the mountain of furs stacked in the corner. "Let me see if I can calm them down."

The wildest of the four horses was the gelding. Will stole quietly to its side and spoke softly to it until it quit whinnying. He rubbed its muzzle and patted its flanks before leading it into the yard. Even then, the horse bucked and kicked each time he tried to load furs on its back. Twice it broke free and had to be chased down. Finally, Mac erupted in anger and planted his fist squarely between the gelding's eyes. The horse emitted a surprised grunt and sank to its knees. The men had no trouble securing their packs on the brute after that.

When the four horses were finally loaded with furs, John Frazer said, "Before you boys go, I have some provisions to get ya."

Frazer led his friends back inside the trad-ing post and took three knapsacks from pegs on the back wall. He crammed each with smoked venison, black rind cheese, a loaf of hard bread, and some handfuls of oats for the horses. Then, John stacked the knapsacks beside the supplies Mac had picked out.

Will, Jack, and Alexander thanked the trader and snatched up their provisions. As they shook hands with John, he told them, "In case ya don't know, Will's Creek is the Ohio Company's base camp. The fella I deal with there is Thomas Jones. His bungalow is right next to the tavern. Good luck! I'll give you those new traps when ya get back."

With a wide grin, Lightnin' again thanked Frazer and then led his party south along the banks of the Monongahela. When he reached the confluence of the Youghiogheny, he and the others followed that river directly south. It was then that one of the chestnut mares kept straying out of line. Over and over Will herded it back on the trail, only to have the rebellious horse bolt into the woods to munch wild leeks. Finally, the lad grabbed its lead rope and MacDonald one of its heavily muscled hind legs to keep it going straight.

"Watch out, Mac, if old Betty tries lifting her tail," joshed Will. "Then, you'll be about the same color she is."

The woodsmen had just gotten the horses moving in good order again when a fierce storm hit them head-on. A driving rain drenched man and beast and slowed their progress to a crawl. Even worse was the hail that raised welts on exposed skin. Finally, Lightnin' howled, "Head fer the hemlocks. Now!"

This time, the men had no trouble getting their charges to move. Off the horses plunged into a dense thicket prodded by the stinging ice. The hail made such a racket smacking the boughs above that the beasts ran fifty yards back into the brush before Will, Jack, and Mac could stop them.

The storm raged for three more hours until the nerves of man and beast alike were stretched to the limit. When the downpour finally slowed and moved off to the east, there was only an hour of daylight left. Finally, the testy MacDonald drove the others from the thicket and growled, "This is na a good place to camp. We best move on. Maybe we'll find a cabin or a cave."

Reluctantly, Will and Jack followed their partner back onto the trail. The deluge had turned it into a mire, and the travelers sunk into muck up to their ankles with each step they took. Instead of finding shelter, they entered a dense forest that hemmed them in like the sides of a tomb. There, huge mountain lion tracks were everywhere, and the horses grew twice as skittish as before. They bucked and snorted and became so unmanageable that finally even MacDonald was in favor of camping for the night.

After examining a vivid, clawed lion print at the side of the trail, Hawkins said, "We best build a roarin' fire. That'll keep them big cats at bay."

"Aye," agreed Mac. "We'll gather lots o' wood to feed it all night. Will, ye can take first watch. I'll relieve ya in a few hours."

"Don't you think I should tend to the horses first?" replied Cutler.

"You're right, laddie. Me brain must already be asleep."

After Will unloaded the furs from the horses' backs, he lovingly cleaned the mud from their coats with a currycomb. Then, he hobbled the animals and fed them handfuls of oats he fetched from his knapsack. MacDonald and Hawkins, meanwhile, snapped a huge mound of dry branches from the trunks of some nearby hemlocks and built a crackling bonfire. They barely finished their chores when darkness crept from the woods to blot out all features of the landscape around them. It was so black that the trees themselves were swallowed up.

"H-H-How did you become a mountain man, Lightnin'?" stammered Will, glancing nervously around him at the all-pervading gloom. "The r-r-rest of us told our stories. W-W-What's yours?"

"Wall now, I sprung up like grass an' have growed wild ever since," replied Jack with a mighty yawn. "Ain't no more to tell even if I weren't bone tired."

"Aye, good night, laddie," grunted Mac. "An' keep that fire a roarin'. Ye hear me?"

"Yes, sir," replied the boy. "See you in a couple of hours."

Completely worn out from their strenuous journey, Mac and Jack collapsed on the damp ground and wound themselves in their blankets. They immediately fell into a dead slumber, leaving Will to his own fears. With a shiver, Cutler tossed more wood on the blaze and drew a little closer to it. Several times he heard furtive movement in the blackness behind him. The horses must have heard it, too, because they snorted nervously until Will added yet more hemlock branches to expand the firelight to where the nervous animals huddled together.

Despite his apprehension, Will's eyelids got heavier and heavier. He stretched his neck, rubbed his cramped legs, and got up to stagger wearily around the fire. When he plopped back down, his head sunk between his shoulders, and his eyes swam with dizziness. To stave off sleep, he hummed a familiar hymn. Then, he thought about Bright Star until almost overcome by his narcotic dream of her. This, in turn, caused him to say his sisters' names aloud: "Mary, Abbey, Judith, Jane, Lizzy, Sarah, Mary, Abbey. . ."

The next thing Will heard was an almost human shriek. He sprang to his feet to find himself in total darkness. Off to his left echoed a fearful snarling and whinnies of fear and distress. It was too dark to find his long rifle, so he drew his knife and rushed toward a sudden struggle that ensued from the black void of night.

Cutler almost reached the desperate neighing of a downed horse when he was bowled over by a powerful shadow. He hit the ground on his back with his muscular adversary on top of him. The beast's hot breath reeking of horse blood made Will gag as he tried to fend it off. All the while sharp claws tore at his clothes and brought stinging pain to his extremities. When the hot breath closed on his throat, a sudden rush of adrenaline caused the lad to strike wildly with his now remembered knife. The blade struck home again and again, causing the creature he grappled to caterwaul and thrash wildly. Finally, after a particularly vicious slash, the beast gave one final shriek and went limp. Its dead weight was suffocating, and Will lost consciousness trying to push it off him.

Cutler woke to the sound of faraway voices. Cautiously, he opened his eyes and found Jack and Mac hovering over him with concern etched on their tan faces. The fire was again burning brightly, and in its eerie glow Will saw the gelding lying nearby with gore leaking from its rent throat. Still on top of him sprawled the tawny form of a great lion slashed in many places with crimson wounds. He started at the sight of it and cried, "G-G-Get him off me! Off me!"

A smile gleamed in Lightnin's beard, and he chuckled, "That rascal won't hurt ya none after ya done stabbed the tar out of 'im. You're a real mountain man now, Will, an' I'm gonna call ya Big Cat Cutler from this day on. Look at the size o' that cuss you ventilated. Why, I'da had my hands full with a lion that huge."

Mac reached down and rolled the dead carcass from Will's chest. Afterward he muttered, "So ye let the fire go out, an' this be the consequence. It's a lucky thing ye aren't the one we be throwin' dirt over instead o' Frazer's horse."

"Don't listen to that sour old Scot," chortled Hawkins. "Can ya get up, Big Cat?"

"I-I-I think so. . ."

"Then, do it!" commanded Alexander.

Cutler rose groggily to his feet and staggered back to the fire. There, Lightnin' examined his wounds and bound the deeper ones with strips of cloth he tore from his extra shirt. "Wagh!" whistled the trapper. "That rascal's claws sure was sharp. Some of yer scratches go clean to the bone."

"It'd be as tough to lose a brother as it was a father," grumbled Mac, putting his arm around Will's shoulder. "Are ye going to be able to walk tomorrow? Now, we'll have to carry those furs the gelding lugged for us. You know that, don't you?"

# CHAPTER TWELVE: WILL'S CREEK

The next morning Will slept until the sun had risen well above the trees. When he slowly returned to consciousness, he felt weak and nauseous. His arms ached, too, and stinging pain ebbed from a multitude of tender places.

When the lad finally sat up, he found Jack and Mac staring at him from across their campfire. The other trappers were gnawing on smoked venison and hard bread. Finally, Hawkins said after swallowing his food, "How's Big Cat doin' this fine day?"

"I-I-I'm pretty sore," replied Cutler, stretching his hard, stringy muscles. "And bleeding, too."

"Aye, those claw wounds won't heal for some time," muttered Alexander. "We best lay up and let you rest."

"An' we got horse buryin' an' lion skinnin' to do, too," reminded Jack. "That lion pelt will make ya a fine cap, Will."

"Can I put its face on the front? That'd sure fit the name you tagged on me."

"You earned that name with yer brav'ry," responded Hawkins. "I had nothin' to do with it."

"Me, brave?" queried Cutler with a broad grin. "I never thought I'd hear those words together."

The trappers spent three more days camped on the fringe of the dense forest to allow Will's wounds to heal. He spent the time soaking up the abundant spring sunshine and repeatedly telling his friends how he killed the lion. By the time they reloaded the horses and headed for Will's Creek, the lad strutted about with his chest puffed out and a cocky smile planted on his face.

Noting Cutler's air of self-importance, Alex said, "It looks like ye better make that lion skin cap a size eight."

"Size eight?" echoed Will.

"Aye, that's the only way it'll fit that swelled head o' yours."

"Ah, let 'im alone," grunted Hawkins. "Every mountaineer has the right to crow a little, 'specially after he's proved hisself a man."

The woodsmen kept a slow pace the first day back on the trail to allow Cutler to get his legs back under him. The horses were sluggish, too, and had to be prodded up each hill and incline. The weather was warmer than usual for that time of year, forcing the thirsty travelers to stop often at the springs they encountered along the way.

At noon the party stopped at a small pond and ate more of the provisions Frazer had provided them. Afterward, Will skipped flat stones across the smooth surface of the pool. Catching a glimpse of his reflection in the water, he gasped at the changes in his appearance since he had escaped from the Indians. His shaven dome was now covered with a flax-colored mop of hair that accented the deep blue of his eyes. His once-scrawny frame had filled out, too, and looked rather powerful to the lad. He struck a series of manly poses to more greatly appreciate his muscularity until Mac said, "You've grown a wee bit, eh, laddie?"

"Yes, I have!" exclaimed Will.

"Then, put them muscles to good use, Adonis, loadin' the packs on the horses. We're a wastin' daylight dawdlin' here."

The next day the party finally emerged from the dense forest into a less rugged land crisscrossed by meadows. The mares became more manageable in the open country, allowing the trappers to break into long, ground-eating strides. Striking off to the southeast, they soon came to the outskirts of a small village of hastily erected log huts.

"Wagh!" bellowed Lightnin'. "We done made it to Will's Creek. An' there's the tavern, jess ahead. I'm buyin' if you fellas is drinkin'."

"I'm drinking!" yelled Will.

"Me, too," said Mac, "after we deliver these furs to Thomas Jones."

The trappers led their pack horses up the narrow, muddy streets to a sprawling, log bungalow that took up half a block next to the tavern. In front of the door sat a squat, jovial fellow puffing on a clay pipe. The trader pushed his tri-corner hat back on his head, and a friendly grin extended his fat cheeks. "You got quite a haul there, fellas," he observed. "Leave any beaver fer next year?"

"Wall now," chortled Lightnin', "that depends on how far you're willin' to lug your traps."

"Be you Jones?" asked Alex.

"I be."

"Then, you're the man John Frazer sent us to find."

"Where's Henry Miller?"

"Dead. That's why Frazer sent us."

"Ah, what a shame," sighed the trader. "Miller was a good, honest man. How did he die?"

"We think the Frenchies got 'im," replied Hawkins. "I'm Jack, by the way, an' this here's Mac an' Will."

"Well, them French will pay once Washington gets here. He's on his way with an army o' Virginians, right now."

"Aye, we met George last winter," said MacDonald. "He was on some mission then, too."

"Well, boys, bring John's plews inside, an' we'll settle up. Does he want paid in gold or in credit?"

"He didn't say," answered Mac. "Credit would be better for us, so we're not responsible for his money. Give us a signed receipt, an' he can make up his own mind when he gets it."

"Good answer. Now, I know why John trusted you."

Hawkins and MacDonald unloaded the horses and dragged the furs inside the trading post. Then, Will rubbed down the mares and fed them some oats. Afterward, he unrolled his cougar skin and stared in awe at the length and breadth of it. As he continued to examine the fine pelt, a burly townsman staggered out of the tavern next door and lurched over to the boy.

"Where'd ya git that fur?" the man slurred, attempting to snatch it from Will's hand.

"Hey, let go!" barked Cutler. "That's mine."

"Not if I kin sell it fer rum, it ain't."

"But I killed that lion. I got the scratches to prove it. See?"

"Ahhhh! Yer mama give ya them fer not hangin' up her washin'," mocked the drunk with a sneer. "Gimme that pelt!"

"Not without a fight," snarled Will.

The lad jerked away his lion skin and heaved it on the doorstep of the trading post. As soon as his head was turned, his antagonist cuffed him with a hard blow that sent Will sprawling.

In an instant Cutler sprang to his feet and charged the belligerent drunk. The man sidestepped at the last instant and stuck out his foot. Will emitted a surprised cry and again found himself on the ground.

Rolling quickly from his stomach to his back, the lad saw his opponent angling toward his pelt. Angrily, he leaped up again and hammered the man with two punches to the face. Blood streamed from the drunk's nose, and a dangerous look gleamed in his eyes. Drawing a knife from his boot, he lunged at Will three times in quick succession. The boy juked and dodged and then drew his own knife.

Seeing the length of Cutler's skinning blade made the man back up until he touched the trading post wall. Will then fired his knife toward the lout's neck, catching him through the coat collar and pinning him neatly to the logs behind him.

No matter how the man struggled, he couldn't free himself and soon his curses of rage turned to pleading. "Let me go," implored the drunk, dropping his own knife on the ground. "I-I-I'm sorry fer b-b-botherin' you, young fella."

"That a way, Big Cat!" howled Lightnin', stepping into the street from the trading post door. "Look at that fella squirm. Why, he looks like a gal that jess seen her first rattler. Let her loose before she stains them britches o' hers."

Cutler kicked away the drunk's knife and then unpinned him from the wall. Will snarled in the man's face, and he turned and ran up the street as fast as his legs would carry him. As he disappeared from sight, Lightnin' said, "Ain't no townsman can best a mountain man. Let's you an' me go to the tavern an' get us a slurp o' rum to celebrate."

"No thanks," replied Big Cat. "If rum'd make me act like that mangy skunk, then I'll have to pass."

"That's tellin' 'im, laddie," said Mac, joining his friends on the street. "What if we go to the tavern an' have us a wee bit o' supper instead?"

"Sure!" agreed Will, stooping to gather up his lion skin. "And a little ale to wash it down."

"Hey, what's that I hear?" asked Lightnin', cocking his ear toward the south. "Is it drummin'?"

"Aye, you're right as rain," replied Alexander. "It must be George Washington's boys a comin'."

The woodsmen turned just in time to see three companies of Virginia militia marching briskly toward them to the smart beat of their drummers. The column was dressed in dark blue coats and marched with a precision that made Will gasp. "Look!" exclaimed the lad. "There's Washington out front. What a fine horse he's riding."

As the column of soldiers reached the outskirts of town, people spewed out of their doorways to greet them. By the time the Virginians had reached the tavern, there was barely enough room for them to pass through the swelling crowd.

"So ya come to kick them Frenchies' behinds?" crowed Hawkins after Washington had dismounted from his white stallion.

"That's the plan," said George stiffly. "Say, I could use you men to do some scouting for me. Are you interested?"

"You bet! Me an' my partners jess come from the French fort. We kin lead ya right to it."

"Aye, we might as well help," agreed Alex, "bein' we can't trap with all those Indians there."

"I'm in!" cried Big Cat. "I wouldn't miss this adventure for anything. I'll go find someone to take care of John's mares while we're gone."

"All right, then," replied Colonel Washington. "Be ready to move out at dawn."

"I jess hope them Frenchies is as easy to skin as the lion Will killed," Lightnin' said. "Look at the size o' his pelt, Colonel."

"That is a monster. Congratulations, Cutler."

"Thank you, sir," mumbled Will. "I reckon I better sell it, though, before we leave in the morning. That hide's just too big to lug very far despite all the memories it has for me."

"At least keep the head, Big Cat," urged Hawkins. "Ya gotta have some trophy ta look at when you're snowed in next winter with nothin' but the past ta feed on."

"Good idea. I'll go back to Jones' place and see what he can do for me."

# CHAPTER THIRTEEN: AN EASY VICTORY

"Some adventure this turned out to be," grumbled Will, rubbing the shoulder he hurt hoisting logs into place in the hastily erected wall.

"Aye," agreed MacDonald. "All we've done is tramp over five mountains, ford two swollen rivers, an' then build this spindly palisade Washington's callin' Fort Necessity."

"But look at all the purty country we seen," teased Hawkins. "An' weren't it fun paddlin' the colonel down the Youghiogheny on a scoutin' mission?"

"All that proved was that the river be too rocky for transportin' cannon an' baggage. An' we almost went over Ohiopyle Falls, to boot!"

"Awww, cheer up, will ya, Mac? With all the couriers runnin' in an' out o' this here camp, we's bound to see action soon."

"Hey, look. There's Christopher Gist," said Alexander, pointing to a tall frontiersman who burst from the woods bordering Great Meadows and rushed toward Washington's tent. "Let's go see what news he's a bringin'."

The woodsmen dropped their axes, grabbed their long rifles, and moseyed over to eavesdrop on the conversation leaking from the canvas walls of the colonel's headquarters. They started cleaning their weapons to fool the sentry posted outside the tent.

"Just yesterday," reported Gist, "fifty Frenchies come to Mount Braddock and pushed their way inta my home. They was lookin' fer you, George, an' made no bones about it. A Monsieur La Force was the fella done all the talkin'."

"Where'd they go?" asked George evenly.

"After I played dumb, they went about their scoutin'. I run across their tracks on my way over. Them tracks was only five mile from here an' mighty recent."

"Then, I'd better warn Tanacharison."

"How's the old Half-King doin'?" Christopher inquired.

"Just the same. We have trouble agreeing on war strategy."

"Well, good luck. I best git back to my plantation before some other unwanted visitors drop by."

Will, Mac, and Jack nodded to Gist when he emerged from Washington's tent and then streaked back into the forest. He had just disappeared when an exhausted Indian runner staggered into camp from the west. The woodsmen rushed to assist the Iroquois and helped him hobble to headquarters. Hearing them approach, the colonel strode outside and said to the courier, "Greetings, my brother. Do you have a message for me?"

"Tanacharison find French enemy. Wants you to meet him. Six mile. That way. I take you."

"Not before you get some rest. Hawkins, you and your friends take our brother over to the supply tent and get him some food and water. Stay with him until he's ready to go."

"Yes, sir."

While Jack, Mac, and Will tended to the Iroquois runner, Washington assembled his small army before the fort. He ordered forty men to stay behind and guard their ammunition. The other one hundred and ten soldiers he aligned in marching formation. When the woodsmen and the Indian guide rejoined them, they immediately set out through the woods to find the Half-King.

The farther Washington's force moved west, the denser the forest got. Soon, they were traveling single file down a narrow path a deer would have had trouble squeezing through. Then, the skies opened to drench the men with a fierce downpour. It soon became so slippery that the soldiers knocked each other down at every turn of the trail.

"What are we, men or tenpins?" groused Mac after being bowled off his feet by a clumsy Virginia soldier.

"With yer hard head, it's tough to tell," laughed Lightnin'.

"I just hope Pearl's barrel isn't full of mud," groused Will, while sliding several feet on his belly.

"Who's Pearl?" grunted the fallen militiaman.

"My rifle, you dunderhead!" snapped Cutler testily. "What'd ya think?"

"Don't get insolent with me, boy!"

"Who you callin' 'boy'?" growled Hawkins. "Why, that's Big Cat Cutler you're talkin' to."

"He don't look so big to me," muttered the Virginian, "but I don't want no trouble. I'm havin' enough problems standin' upright without crossin' no mountain men on top of it."

Washington's party still had not reached the Half-King's camp when night fell. Soon, it became so incredibly dark that the soldiers spent more time relocating the trail than they did traveling on it. For hours they fought the rain and darkness until they finally spied several dim campfires just ahead.  Upon spotting the firelight, Washington hissed his men to silence and sent Hawkins ahead to reconnoiter.

With his heart in his throat, Lightnin' stole noiselessly through the pitch blackness.  He knew that one fall on the muddy path would betray the position of his whole party.  He wasn't sure if the French or Iroquois were ahead, so he slunk forward a half-step at a time with his eyes probing the night.  He detected no sentries and wondered if he might not be leading Washington into a trap.

On and on Lightnin' crept until he was within fifty feet of the encampment.  It was then that an Iroquois rose from his blankets and stretched by the fire.  Hawkins called out to the Indian in his own language.   After the brave acknowledged him, Jack stepped out of the darkness and shouted for Washington to advance.

At the sound of Jack's voice, Tanacharison also stood and waited for the colonel's arrival.  The Half-King was tall and well-built.  From the firelight dancing off his face, Jack guessed him to be around fifty.  He had a dangerous look about him that made Hawkins glad he was friendly to the English.

Tanacharison and Washington greeted one another and then conferred until the first glimmer of morning.  The chief made several drawings in the damp earth near his campfire that did not please George.  Finally, the colonel nodded his approval to the Half-King's fifth battle plan.  Immediately after, the Iroquois filed off into the brush with the colonials tagging behind.  "Not one sound!" warned Washington as they followed the stealthy warriors into the undergrowth.

The allies arrived at the foot of a steep mountain, which they nimbly scaled. When they reached the summit, Tanacharison's Indians took the left flank, while Washington deployed his troops to the right. Dropping to their bellies, they slithered forward toward a rocky glen several yards ahead.

Peering into the hollow, Hawkins could just make out a few soldiers, dressed in sky-blue waistcoats, milling about cooking breakfast. Their jovial jabbering drifted to him with the smell of roasting venison. Their arms were stacked near each campfire, and they appeared totally unaware of anything but their growling bellies.

Hawkins continued to crawl ahead, being careful not to bang his gunstock on the rocks. He now was so close he could see the moustached faces of the enemy. Moving his right hand an inch at a time, he carefully poured some fresh priming powder into the pan of his long rifle. He had just cocked his piece when he saw Washington rise to his knees and take aim at one of the officers below. George's rifle exploded with a loud clap of thunder that echoed repeatedly through the enemy hideaway, sending the French marines scrambling for their muskets.

Jack saw that Washington's target was down, and he sought another officer to fire at. He spotted a captain's pin on a Frenchman's waistcoat and drew a bead on his chest. The roar of his rifle was followed by the bark of the men's weapons around him, and it became too smoky to see if his bullet had found its mark. Rotely, he loaded his musket and searched for another blue coat below.

The French were firing exclusively at Hawkins and his mates, which allowed Tanacharison's Iroquois to creep even closer. Finally, with blood-curdling whoops, the Indians leaped from hiding, wielding their hatchets with deadly effect. Jack sat transfixed watching the warriors hack down the surprised foe. The battle was over in a few minutes after that when the remaining marines threw down their guns and raised their hands as a sign of surrender.

Hawkins glanced at Will and Mac and found similar grim looks etched on their powder-begrimed faces. Neither looked very happy over winning the brief battle. Instead, they watched in ghastly silence as the Iroquois scalped the dead Frenchmen littering the rocky ground below.

Colonel Washington, meanwhile, rose from his point of ambush and said with a thin smile, "I have heard the bullets whistle, and, believe me, there is something charming to the sound. Forward, men, and gather up the prisoners."

As Lightnin' slipped down the mountainside, he saw one of the marines bolt for an opening in the rocks. He whipped his rifle to his shoulder and squeezed off a quick shot. The hammer fell with a dull thud, and then he realized in the excitement of battle that he had forgotten to reload his piece. He leaped forward to catch the fleeing soldier but slipped on the rain-glazed rock and fell hard on his back. By the time his breath returned to him, the Frenchman had disappeared down a steep incline and scrambled into the woods.

The Iroquois were still too busy scalping their ten dead enemies to pay the fleeing soldier any mind. When they were finished hacking the hair from the felled men, Tanacharison gathered up the bloody trophies and pulled a string of black wampum from his possibles bag. These he handed to a runner and said in broken English for all to hear, "Take to tribes of Ohio. Tell them of our easy victory. Tell them to fight these French who build forts on our land."

After the Half-King had spoken, Washington descended into the glen and shouted, "Get those prisoners in line. Are there any officers left among them?"

"Oui, monsieur," said a short, rattled lieutenant, stepping from the ranks. "I am LaForce, and I request that you bury our commander before ze Iroquois mutilate him further."

"And who may that be?" asked the colonel.

"Sieur de Jumonville. Over there he lay."

"Hawkins, Cutler, take care of that for me."

"Yes, sir," muttered Jack, "but his grave'll be mighty shallow in this rocky soil. Let's go, Big Cat. We got some diggin' to do."

As Jack and Will carried out Washington's order, Cutler said, "You know, I came out here hoping to be a hero to impress Bright Star. I thought I'd shoot so many Frenchies that Tanacharison would go back to Logstown and tell everyone about me. I shot one man, and all I got out of it was a sick feeling in my stomach."

"Killin' ain't never purty, Will, but sometimes a fella is forced into it by things out o' his control. Be glad ya lived through this here battle an' ain't turned sour like Mac did after Culloden. Look at 'im over there by hisself. His face is as hard as the rock he's settin' on."

# CHAPTER FOURTEEN: A WORSE DEFEAT

Mac became even more withdrawn after Washington's army returned to Fort Necessity. He only spoke when spoken to and answered with an "Aye" or "Na." He didn't gripe once when ordered to help finish the palisade or enlarge the entrenchment. Food was scarce now, too, but that also elicited no response from the doughy Scotchman.

One bright morning Washington held a grand ceremony to give Tanacharison an English name. When all the speech-giving and fanfare still did not boost Alex's spirits, Hawkins said to him, "The battle we jess fought musta brung back some bad memories for ya, eh, Mac?"

"Aye, I've been relivin' a lot o' bloodshed," MacDonald confessed. "It was all them guns a firin'. . ."

"Then, it's time to let it go, brother," cajoled Lightnin', putting his arm around his friend's shoulder. "We all got struggles to face an' demons to beat. Look at how much Big Cat here has overcome."

"Yes, cheer up," urged Will. "We really need your help to get through our next tussle with the Frenchies. You know that, don't you?"

Alex again lapsed into silence as he mulled over his pals' words. "I-I-I be alright now," he stammered after a moment. "Sure, I'll help. I be the one with the most soldierin' experience, even if it do make me crazy."

Mac, Will, and Jack all breathed a little easier when new militia units began streaming into Great Meadows daily. Washington's forces soon swelled to 400 men, and the colonel held strategy meetings with his officers and the Half-King to plot their next move. After one such council, Hawkins saw Tanacharison stride scowling from headquarters. Washington appeared soon after, his face as red as his hair. "Get the men assembled," he barked. "We're moving to Gist's plantation to prepare for the French."

A rash of grumbling accompanied the colonel's announcement. Soon, the soldiers and Indians found themselves plunging through the dense forest. The terrain was so rough that the men tripped and fell more than they marched. Many of the colonials lugged heavy baggage that snagged in the undergrowth and slowed them even further. Finally, Mac howled in frustration, "This brush be takin' all the fight out o' us. By the time we reach Gist's, we'll already be beat!"

"That's what I like to hear," chortled Lightnin', slapping MacDonald on the back, "some nice normal complainin'."

"The Half-King must agree with Alex," panted Will, pointing toward the Iroquois. "Look, he's turning his braves back to Great Meadows."

Wearily, Washington's army staggered on until they reached the base of Laurel Hill. Here, the footing became even more rocky and treacherous and progress slowed to a crawl. It wasn't until two weeks later that the force finally fought their way over the high ground and stumbled out of the woods at Mount Braddock.

"Boy, what a march that was," puffed Cutler when they drew up in formation to answer roll call.

"Aye, that be the toughest thirteen miles I've ever tramped," agreed Mac, mopping his brow with a coarse handkerchief. "On normal ground we'da come that far in one day."

"Silence in the ranks," bellowed Colonel Washington. "It's time to dig entrenchments, men. The French can't be far off now, and we have to be ready."

The soldiers sweated and grunted and cursed their commander until nightfall halted their labor. The next day they still made little headway gouging in the stony earth with knives, hatchets, and a few wooden shovels borrowed from Gist's outbuilding. They hadn't eaten bread in eight days, which sapped their endurance for hard work even further. By late afternoon Will's face grew deathly pale, and his head swam with dizziness. Finally, he was forced to stagger into the shade where dozens of other soldiers had fainted from fatigue.

The entrenchments had just begun to take shape when several scouts scrambled back to Mount Braddock to report a large force of French and Indians moving their way. Seeing the deplorable condition of his men and their scant fortifications, Washington conferred briefly with his officers and then shouted, "Get ready to retreat. Captain Mackay, impress those pack horses I saw in the barn. We'll make better time if they haul our supplies."

"So Washington has a wee lick o' sense, after all," muttered Mac. "Now, if he could just get us some manna like Moses did for his people in the Wilderness."

Going downhill with pack horses allowed Washington's troops to return to Great Meadows in only three days. As they staggered into Fort Necessity, Will groaned to Jack and Mac, "I think you boys lost a few pounds. You look like scarecrows that escaped from Gist's cornfield."

"An' I got 'bout as much starch left in me," grumbled Alex. "I hope we don't grapple with those Frenchies today, or they scatter our shucks all over this battlefield."

Colonel Washington set his men to felling trees and building a breastwork to strengthen his defensive position. After that, they waited in tense silence for the enemy to arrive. By evening the sky boiled with dark clouds, and a keening wind set the soldiers' nerves on edge. When a trader raced in from the woods to report the French were at Gist's Plantation, the Half-King had had enough. With the Iroquois in his wake, he filed off into the forest without one word of explanation for his obvious desertion.

The next morning an eerie foreboding surrounded the fort. The storm clouds grew even thicker above them, and the woods were masked with shadow. Soon after dawn a wounded scout approached, accompanied by a smattering of rain. "I seen nine hundred Indians and Frenchies," he babbled. "Mebbe more. . ."

"Alright, men," commanded Washington, "form up in that open ground before the fort. Leave those trenches, I say."

Dumbfounded, his soldiers crawled to their feet and drew up in two lines in front of the breastworks. The front row knelt to allow those behind them to fire over their heads. When the whole force was thus exposed, Will wondered aloud, "What's going on? Why did we build the blasted fort if we're not going to use it?"

"Washington's just baitin' the French into leaving the woods. If they stay in the trees, we'll never get a clear shot at 'em," explained Mac.

"Wagh! Here they come!" yelped Hawkins. "Burn powder!"

"No, hold your fire!" growled the colonel. "Wait for the enemy to charge."

Lightnin's face reddened at the rebuff, and he gritted his teeth as he watched the French and Indians swarm to the edge of the forest and then pull back. It seemed that behind every tree crouched a white coat or a buckskin hunting shirt. Soon, puffs of smoke rose from the enemy muskets as they unleashed a ragged fire at the Virginians. In the next instant, Hawkins saw a half-dozen colonials tumble from the ranks around him.

Instead of ordering his men to shoot back, Washington barked, "Retreat! Retreat!"

"You bet I will!" cried Jack. "Come on, Big Cat. Mac."

The colonials broke rank and ran toward their trenches, while the French continued to snipe at them. The ground was littered with dead and wounded before they reached their fortification.

Hawkins dove to safety and then searched for a target in the woods behind him. There was now so much musket smoke that he couldn't see anything. The enemy was content to keep it that way because they never did charge across the open ground to take the fort by storm. A heavy rain began to fall, too, until the trenches were half-filled with water. The torrential downpour dampened the black powder and made many muskets too wet to shoot. When the French could not find a soldier to fire at, they began knocking down the Virginians' horses and cattle. By nightfall, Jack saw that all the animals were dead.

Musket flashes continued to puncture the darkness when Will said, "This wasn't much of a battle. All I did was shoot into the trees until my rifle quit working. How about you boys?"

"Aye, I never saw one Frenchie all day. I aimed for their muzzle blasts an' hoped for the best," grunted Mac.

"I ain't shot since the deluge started," added Lightnin'. "I'm keepin' my powder fer huntin' once we git ourselves out o' this mess. Now, if I'd quit shiverin' like a bald goat, I'd be all set."

"This isn't what I'd call a warm summer rain, either," added Will through chattering teeth.

The sporadic gunfire continued until a French officer stepped from the woods and walked toward the fort waving a white flag. Jack heard him shout in English, "Don't shoot, Anglais. Monsieur DeVilliers wishes to parley with your colonel."

"Don't come any closer," warned Washington.

"Then send an officer to discuss terms, monsieur. We guarantee his safety."

"Captain Van Braam go with this man," said Washington after a long silence. "Listen carefully. I don't want anything lost in the translation."

Jack, Mac, and Will lie shivering in the trenches for what seemed like hours before they saw Van Braam sloshing toward them across the drowned plain between the fort and the black woods. He splashed through the gate and immediately huddled with his colonel to discuss the French terms of surrender.

"DeVilliers will allow us to leave with the honors of war," Hawkins heard the captain say. "We in turn must surrender our cannon and admit responsibility for the death of Jumonville in the action of May 28th."

"We're outnumbered two to one," sighed Colonel Washington. "We have no choice but accept this offer."

The next morning loomed black as the previous one, but fortunately the rain had finally stopped. Washington assembled his forces at first light, and they marched from the fort flying their regimental colors. With all the pack animals dead, the troops were forced to carry the fort stores and other baggage. As they passed between the drawn-up French ranks, Will muttered, "What about our dead? Why didn't the colonel ask to bury them before we marched off? What will happen to them now?"

"The Indians'll scalp 'em, an' the crows an' wolves'll take care o' the rest," grunted Lightnin'.

"Speakin' of the Indians, why aren't they here to see us leave?"

"They probably deserted like the Half-King," suggested Mac.

"An' any other fella smart enough to think o' it," concluded Hawkins.

The colonials dejectedly entered the trail leading to Will's Creek. Many limped from their wounds, while the others stumbled half-asleep in an exhausted daze. They had barely reached the forest when they saw flames lick the sky behind them. A groan rose from the ranks at the sight of the great fire caused by the French torching Fort

Necessity. It was then, as if by magic, that a hundred Indians appeared from the brush around them and rushed forward to rummage through the soldiers' packs.

"Look at these varmints," yelped Lightnin', fending off a warrior with the butt end of his long rifle. "They're breakin' the rules o' surrender."

"What tribe is this?" snarled Alex, pushing away another brave.

"Algonquins from Canada. Look at their moose hide moccasins."

"Boy, the French have all the Indians against us!" cried Will.

"Then, it's time to slip into the bushes," urged Jack. "Nobody'll miss us in this mob."

Colonel Washington drew his sword and smacked two Algonquins with the flat of it. "Burn the supplies," he shouted. "Don't let the Indians get our powder."

"Or our scalps, neither," mumbled Hawkins as he led his friends into the laurel.

# CHAPTER FIFTEEN: THE RING HUNT

After Jack, Mac, and Will slipped from Washington's army, they spent the rest of the day foraging for food. With the woods alive with Algonquins, they dared not fire at deer, so they gorged themselves on strawberries and the shoots of stinging nettle. One man always watched, while the others munched delicious plants and berries.

Just before dark the mountaineers found a secluded grove of hemlocks in which to hole up. It was then that Will made a sling out of strips of tanned deer hide and killed two roosting grouse with it. As Hawkins and MacDonald built a small, inconspicuous fire to cook the birds, the lad carefully plucked them and saved the feathers to use on arrows.

The next morning Cutler rose earlier than his exhausted friends to build a survival bow. With his knife he cut a limb from a sassafras tree that would serve as his stave. Then, he cut flat, even strips down the belly of the bow. When satisfied with its flexibility and look, he cut both ends cleanly and sliced nocks an inch in from each tip. For a bowstring he twisted together several strands of fishing line. This, he attached to the nocks to test the pull of his bow. To make arrows, he cut some thin, straight willow wands and sharpened the front ends. He notched the back end of the arrows and lashed three feathers on each of them with grouse sinew. The sinew he glued with hemlock pitch for added strength.

Will slipped into the brush with his new weapon and practiced shooting at a rotten stump until he consistently stuck his arrows in it at twenty paces. Soon after, he saw a rabbit hop up the trail in front of him. Creeping a step at a time, he closed within thirty yards when the hare stopped to nibble some grass. Seeming to sense his presence, the hare suddenly took two more nervous hops, forcing Will to fire. He nocked an arrow and let it fly in the same motion, catching his prey just behind the front shoulder. As the lad gathered up the still-kicking hare, he saw another browsing in a patch of clover.

Cutler returned an hour later with three fat rabbits. These he cooked over the coals of the fire until their succulent odor roused his pals from their slumber. "Wagh!" exclaimed Lightnin' when he sat up and saw the roasting game. "An' here I done thought I dreamed this fine breakfast."

"No, I shot them with this," said Will, holding up his bow. "At least I learned something useful keeping the coons out of the Ottawas' corn patch."

After they had eaten, the trappers moved stealthily north until they saw smoke rising from the woods ahead. Slowing their pace even further, they stole to the edge of a familiar clearing and saw Gist's plantation reduced to a smoldering ruin.

"Looks like the Frenchies want all our settlers out o' the Alleghenies," muttered Mac. "I'll bet they burned out John Frazer, too."

"Then, we best head back to our secret trappin' valley," replied Hawkins. "That's the only safe place left."

"Sure, if we can sneak past all the Indians the Frenchies got looking for us," mumbled Cutler.

"That's no attitude to have, Big Cat," scolded Lightnin'. "There ain't a savage alive that's equal to a mountain man, an' don't you fergit it!"

The trappers searched the burned plantation for survivors but found only a few charred bodies. After digging some hasty graves, they again drifted north, giving the Forks of the Ohio a wide berth. The going was extremely tough squeezing through hemlock thickets that slowed their progress to a crawl. Finally, after a week of such travel, they came out on the banks of the Kiskiminetas River.

Yelping with joy, Will threw off his sweaty clothes and dove into the nearest pool. "Wagh! Does that feel good," cried the lad when he resurfaced.

"An' here I thought you was afraid o' water after them Ottawa gals initiated ya," teased Lightnin'.

"Hey, why not wash your clothes while you're at it?" laughed Alex, tossing Cutler's buckskins into the pool after him. "No use gettin' all cleaned up an' then put on filthy duds."

After the woodsmen had bathed and frolicked in the Kiskiminetas, they stumbled upon a wide meadow that made a perfect campsite. Exhausted from their long hike, the trappers made a hasty dinner out of a possum Cutler killed with his bow. Then, they curled up under the stars and fell instantly asleep.

The next morning, Hawkins started awake as a dense cloud of smoke billowed over him. Choking violently, he shook Cutler and MacDonald until they sat up gasping for air. The fringes of the meadow around them were engulfed in flames that moved steadily inward each time the wind breathed from the distant trees.

"What the heck's happenin'?" coughed Mac.

"Looks like a ring hunt," wheezed Will. "Indians set a circle of grass on fire to drive hiding deer out into the open. The Ottawas used it. Often."

"So them skunks is waitin' outside the ring, are they? Then, we best run faster than singed bucks if we's to get outta here," uttered Hawkins.

"But you know how slow I be," mourned Alexander.

"Well, we can't stay here," babbled Cutler, "or we'll burn!"

"How 'bout if I draw their fire, while you fellas sneak around 'em?" suggested Lightnin'. "They'll never hit me 'cause all they'll see is a blur."

"It's worth a try," said Mac, tying a handkerchief around his mouth and nose. "Let's go!"

The three trappers crawled on their bellies to stay below the smoke. Just before they reached the blazing grass, Hawkins pointed ahead toward an obscure chief who fired at a herd of deer bounding out of the flames. His shot knocked down the lead doe, and he waved his arms to chase the animals toward another hunter who peeked out from behind a tree trunk.

The second Indian blasted a small spike buck and immediately charged forward to gut his kill and feast on the liver. When the hunter bent to slit open the deer's belly, Lightnin' scrambled to his feet and was in full flight in less than two strides. As Hawkins burst into the open woods, a surprised whoop greeted him, followed by three wild shots from other concealed braves. With his body bent at the waist, he weaved between the tree trunks running effortlessly.

All the hunters but the chief leaped up to chase Jack. When they disappeared from view, Will and Mac charged from the smoke to rush the remaining Indian, who still hadn't reloaded his musket. When they almost reached him, he spun around and fixed them with a malicious glare that caused them to gasp in surprise and fear. It was Bold Wolf who had shot the first doe!

Before the woodsmen could recover from their shock, Bold Wolf whipped a second rifle to his shoulder and fired at Mac. The bullet creased Alexander's left temple, spinning him to the ground. The Ottawa yanked a hatchet from his belt and leaped forward to finish his foe. It was then that Will planted his rifle butt firmly in the big Indian's chest. Bold Wolf recoiled at the impact, and the lad laid him out with another swift blow to the side of the head. When the Ottawa collapsed to the ground, MacDonald shrilled, "Finish him, laddie. Do it!"

Will cocked his long rifle and pointed the barrel at the unconscious chief's heart. Sweat ran down his forehead and into his eyes until he let down the hammer and said, "I can't kill a defenseless man. It ain't right."

"Defenseless?" screamed Mac, clutching his bleeding temple. "Why he'da scalped me in a minute if you hadn'ta stopped him."

"We can still have our revenge," howled the lad, pointing to the two dead deer. "Let's grab that smaller one and find Jack."

Will hoisted the spike buck onto his shoulders and wrapped its legs around his neck. In the next instant, he and Alex bolted into the woods away from the wildfire still raging across the meadow. Finding themselves on the same trail taken by Jack and his pursuers, they veered off to the right into the densest brush they could find. There, they crept silently along until they heard three short owl hoots. In the next instant Lightnin' appeared at their side with a wide grin peeking from his dark beard. "Lost them Ottawas half-mile back," he whispered gleefully. "An' look. Weren't that nice o' 'em to provide us a buck fer supper?"

"Let's get out o' here," hissed Mac, holding a handkerchief over his wounded temple. "That's Bold Wolf's band we're up against."

The smile faded from Jack's face, and he led them into denser brush still. It was rocky there, too, and the mountain men jumped carefully from one boulder to the next to throw off any trackers. Next, they found a little stream leading west. This they waded for a good mile before traversing yet more rocky ground. By then, Will began to tire, so Lightnin' carried the buck until dusk. When it became too dark to go any farther, they lie down in the brush, taking turns watching for Indians.

At first light the woodsman were again on the move. They put another five miles between them and the Ottawas before holing up in a cave. There, they finished cleaning the buck and impatiently fried some steaks over a small fire. As they gobbled down the half-raw meat, Jack said, "If we ever git separated ag'in, head fer the Allegheny. We got our canoe stashed there an' kin make a fast escape."

"That's a good plan," seconded Mac. "These dense woods be a real threat with all the red men about to ambush us."

"Amen!" agreed Will. "I'm afraid we still haven't seen the last of those devils. After we eat, we better be on our way again."

"Bold Wolf's as dang'rous as any rattler," grunted Hawkins. "Who knows what rock he'll slither out from under next? An' I swear he had a couple o' Delawares with him this time. That's bad news fer every English fella livin' on the frontier."

Reenactor, Joseph Rearick, portrays a Delaware warrior. Most Delawares remained neutral to see if the French or English would gain control of the Alleghenies.

# CHAPTER SIXTEEN: THE GAUNTLET

When Mac, Will, and Jack left the cave, they struck out again for their secret beaver paradise. It was now the hottest part of summer, and the mosquitoes and black flies descended upon them every time they broke into a sweat. Finally, Hawkins stopped on the banks of a gurgling stream and smeared every visible part of his body with a thick coating of mud. Only his eyes showed after he daubed it on his face.

"There's one fellow you best not take a courtin' with you when ye next see Bright Star," chuckled Alexander.

"Hey, at least those gallinippers won't be pesterin' me no more," replied Jack testily.

"Nor squaws, either," Cutler joked.

The trappers saw no more of the Ottawas, but several times they strayed across their moccasin tracks. The Indians seemed to be crisscrossing the countryside trying to find them, so again Hawkins suggested they lay low. This time they chose an island in the middle of a swamp for their hideout. That way, they left no signs coming and going from camp. The mosquitoes, though, were twice as bad there, and it wasn't long before Will and Mac were plastered with mud to fend off the bloodsucking pests.

The woodsmen spent the rest of the summer at their island retreat. When the first autumn leaves began to change colors, Lightnin' said, "If we's gonna git any beaver this fall, we best go back to our valley. This is when the plews are at their finest. We won't be able to buy no powder an' such if we don't trap. Then, we'll really be in a pickle."

"Do you think it's safe?" asked Will, his brow wrinkling with worry.

"We'd better try," sighed MacDonald, "or we'll be out of supplies before the spring thaw."

Reluctantly, the woodsmen waded from the swamp and struck off to the northeast. It grew colder with each passing day, and their breath hung in plumes in the frosty air as they tramped along. Each night they camped in the shelter of rocks or curled up in the dense laurel. To avoid attracting Indians, they made no fires on their cold journey through the wilderness.

One morning Jack woke to a fresh coating of snow on the ground. Rousing his shivering friends, he said, "Maybe we best build a small blaze an' make us some pine needle tea. Don't want to git sick before we reach our trappin' grounds."

"Aye, let's get crackin', Will," agreed Alexander. "I'll gather wood if you'll fill your possibles bag with needles."

"And I'll get some water from that spring over yonder," offered Cutler through chattering teeth. "What are you going to do, Lightnin'?"

"Dig us a fire pit, o' course."

The hunters hustled about doing their chores and then sat soaking up the heat of their campfire. As they sipped on bitter tea, they heard a turkey gobble on a near hillside. When another bird answered down the ridge, Will whispered, "Did you hear that? If I could shoot a big tom, I'd have feathers to make some real arrows. Then, I could build a bow that'd silently kill all the deer we need."

"Let me see what I kin do," answered Hawkins. "This fresh snow'll make trackin' them buggers mighty easy."

"It'll make it easier for them to spot you, too," cautioned Mac. "You know what keen eyesight they have."

"Hey, I wanna go," interrupted Will. "It was my idea."

"No, one man'll have a better chance o' sneakin' up on the flock," insisted Jack. "Those feathers are worth riskin' a rifle shot fer, but two shots might bring unwanted guests."

"Alright, we'll be a glad to rest here by the fire, while ye try your luck," said Alex.

"Hey, and bring back the whole bird, not just the feathers," heckled Cutler. "They wouldn't make very good eatin', you know."

After chortling good-naturedly at Will's gibe, Hawkins grabbed his long rifle and stole off into the brush. He moved stealthily toward the last place he had heard the soft "turk, turk, turk" emit from the hillside. Slipping from tree to tree, it took him a half-hour to cover three hundred yards. All the extra diligence paid off when he spied fifteen greenish bronze birds feeding in the beech just ahead. There were two huge gobblers, several hens, and a gaggle of just-grown chicks.

Jack froze behind an oak to let his excited heartbeat decelerate. After what seemed like forever, he peered carefully around the tree to find a bird to shoot at. What he saw was a suspicious hen coming directly toward him through the ferns. Her head bobbed aggressively as she assumed a herky-jerky strut meant to drive an encroaching predator away from her brood.

Lightnin', then, had no choice but to whip up his rifle and shoot the pesky hen. At the first motion of his long gun, the turkey squawked loudly enough for the whole countryside to hear. In the next instant she erupted in flight and came straight for Jack's head. He dove to the ground just before her wings brushed him, accidentally discharging his piece.

After the roar of his long rifle echoed off down the hill, Hawkins rose red-faced to slap the snow from his buckskins. He filled the air with curses as he rammed another charge down his gun barrel and watched the rest of the turkeys take flight. Then, he stalked off angrily in the same direction the turkeys had flown. The sun had come up now, filling the woods with hazy light. Naturally, the birds had escaped directly east, making Lightnin' squint as he rushed along the ridge.

The woodsman broke into a trot until he found where the turkeys had lighted in the snow. He examined their wing marks with a broad grin. The grin disappeared quickly when he saw that their new tracks seemed to double back through a heavy thicket to where he had originally kicked them out not more than an hour ago.

Cursing in frustration, Jack spun on his heels and started after the flock. He fought his way through the thick brush until he again reentered the familiar beech woods. There, he suddenly became very tired from his brisk walk and the late morning heat. "Better stop an' rest," he muttered to himself. "Unless I slows my pace, I'll scare them buggers off ag'in."

Hawkins took a seat at the base of a gnarled tree and let the sunshine bake into him. He closed his eyes and drifted off into a pleasant dream where he roasted three turkeys at once over a huge bonfire that warmed him to the marrow of his bones. Mac and Will were there, too, munching on huge drumsticks with turkey juice dripping down their happy faces. He reached out to carve off a drumstick of his own when a very near gobble startled him back to reality. A rush of excitement pulsed through his veins, and he fought the impulse to leap to his feet. Not wishing to flush this bird, he eked open his eyes to search for the turkey that had roused him.

Instead of spying a fat gobbler, Jack found himself encircled by menacing Ottawas and Delawares. Snarls contorted their fierce, painted faces, and they took turns prodding him with their musket barrels until he rose to his feet. Hawkins knew if he showed any sign of fear, the savages would kill him on the spot. He immediately curled his own lips in a defiant sneer and stood with his rifle folded tightly in the crook of his left arm.

When a Delaware brave stepped forward to snatch away his gun, the trapper barked, "No one touches Little Lightnin'! Back off!"

The sudden fury of Jack's voice startled the Indian, and he leaped away in surprise. Before Hawkins could intimidate the brave further, a muscular chief swung his war club and clocked Hawkins on the side of the head. The woodsman staggered with the blow and reeled into a row of Indians, who grabbed wildly at his rifle until it slipped from his grasp. Another clubbing knocked him to the ground, and he heard a rush of black wings pour in his ear hole.

The red men had now burst into a joyous series of shrill cries followed by a familiar long victory whoop. Recognizing the latter as the scalp halloo, Lightnin' leaped woozily to his feet and growled, "You don't scare me. I'm Lightnin' Jack Hawkins, the fiercest mountain man in these here parts. Wall, I'm faster 'n' the West Wind an' more powerful 'n' a rockslide. Mess with me, an' I bury ya under!"

Jack's outburst again silenced the Ottawas and Delawares. When his vision cleared, he saw them staring at him blankly until their chief derided them with a guttural tongue lashing. Then, the braves immediately rushed Jack and began dragging him by man-force down the hill. They smacked him repeatedly as they pulled him along. Glancing back, the trapper saw that their chief was none other than Bold Wolf.

Hawkins continued to struggle until the Indians stopped hitting him. He soon learned this was a mistake because one brawny brave then lassoed him with a stout rope. This allowed his captors to pull him at their will, and the athletic red men immediately broke into a lope that would have matched any deer in the forest. Jack easily kept pace, though, and was content that at least the Indians no longer thumped him.

The party continued to run for two straight hours without stopping. Finally, they came to a creek running due west. They followed this small stream to a large brook that cascaded in many falls down a rocky hillside. The Indians broke stride and moved carefully down the incline to the forest floor below. There, they again sprinted forward until Jack saw the banks of the Allegheny through the trees.

Bold Wolf led his band upriver for several miles until they came to a meadow that stretched to the river's edge. Many Ottawas, Delawares, and Shawnees camped there, and Hawkins' captors raised the scalp halloo to alert the Indians ahead. Immediately after, the encampment rang with whoops, shrill shrieks, and the firing of rifles. When Jack was dragged into the center of this hubbub, he thought all the fiends of hell had been set loose.

Upon spying the trapper, the Indians rapidly formed two lines. Brandishing hatchets, switches, ramrods, rifles, and war clubs, they beckoned him to run through their midst. They spit and howled and worked themselves into such a frenzy that even Jack was a little shaken. Many of the warriors he recognized as those he and Mac had tricked at Venango. Others were part of the hunting party Will had stolen the deer from. Yes, and there was Chief Deep Waters, ugly scar and all, whom he had chased from Frazer's Trading Post. It seemed that all his old nemeses had shown up together to bash him into jam. The Indians called this little party "running the gauntlet." After surveying the hissing, snarling faces, Hawkins pinched himself twice to make sure he wasn't dreaming this whole episode.

Jack took one more long look at the warriors who waited to club him. Many were painted a hideous black that enhanced their demon-like appearance. Their faces, too, were contorted fiendishly as they howled for him to begin. Equally disturbing were the three guards who stood beyond the gauntlet to make sure he didn't escape if he did survive this torture. One was an old Delaware chief who stood with a musket cradled in the crook of his arm. The others held deadly spears decorated with eagle feathers.

Suddenly, the trapper was pushed from behind to prod him into running. Wheeling in anger, he saw Bold Wolf leering evilly at him. "So who fiercest mountain man, now?" taunted the chief. "Can't be he who cower like fawn or frightened kit."

"Let me loose, an' you'll find out quick-like!" snarled Jack, squirming to free himself from the lasso that still bound him. "How kin I run proper like this?"

Hawkins continued to rage and struggle until one of his tormentors stepped forward to cut him free with a flint knife. The instant he was untied, Lightnin' slammed his fist into Bold Wolf's sneering smile, spraying blood and teeth in all directions. Then, he whirled and sprinted for all he was worth between the lines of gasping Indians.

In just two strides Jack was already running full-speed. He flew so fast that he got halfway through the gauntlet before the savages could react. As he streaked along, he juked and dodged and roared like a man possessed. Finally, a powerful Delaware swung a huge war club that just missed Hawkins' ear. The momentum of the swing carried the weapon back into the line of Indians, braining the unlucky brave beside him. Hawkins cackled at the mishap, incensing another warrior to swing so hard that his hatchet slipped from his grasp. When it missed the elusive trapper, the axe sailed into the row of Indians across from him, severely wounding a tall Ottawa.

Lightnin' then began to vary his speed to throw off his attackers. By slowing down or streaking faster, he ruined the aim of another dozen assailants. Outraged by this maneuver, two Shawnees who faced each other swung simultaneously at the woodsman. At the last second Jack ducked, and the Indians knocked each other out. Hawkins had little time to relish this victory, however, when a brawny brave smacked him across the face with his ramrod. This stung so much that he didn't have time to evade a rifle stock that hit him in the stomach. Jack went down in a heap as again the Indians raised a rapid succession of piercing shrieks.

As the Shawnees there closed in for the kill, Jack scooped up a handful of dirt. Leaping to his feet, he flung the debris in the eyes of his nearest enemies. The braves screeched in frustration and sudden pain and groped blindly for Hawkins as he wormed through their midst. Only Deep Waters wasn't affected. With a shrill whoop, he swung his hatchet with all his might. Just before it struck Jack between his shoulder blades, a dazed Shawnee stumbled into its path. The ax sliced through the ill-fated brave's neck, showering his tribesmen with gore. The resulting confusion allowed Hawkins to squeeze into the last stretch of the gauntlet.

Now, only ten Indians stood between Jack and freedom. With a determined scowl, he raced ahead, ignoring the blows that rained upon him. Just as he was to burst from the double file of whooping Indians, a stout Ottawa stepped squarely in his path to block his flight. The brave was swinging Jack's own long rifle to bowl him off his feet. He was too wide to dart around and too well-armed to attack. Just when all looked lost, a shot rang out, and the Ottawa collapsed backward with a neat bullet hole in his forehead.

Jack pushed past the smitten brave. Snatching his gun out of midair, he blasted the last hatchet-wielding warrior at the end of the gauntlet. Immediately, two guards rushed forward to spear him. As Hawkins fended off the first sentinel with his rifle stock, the second thrust his lance at the trapper's exposed ribs. The spear point was just about to pierce Jack's flesh when a second shot tore through the Indian's hand, snapping his weapon in half.

Jack hit the first Indian with a lightning-quick thrust of his rifle butt, knocking him senseless. Then, he laid out the wounded guard with a swift blow to the head. In the next instant, he was streaking for the forest past the old Indian chief. The sachem threw his musket to his shoulder and drew a steady bead on Hawkins' disappearing back. Before his musket could spit fire, a third shot echoed from the forest to take him through the heart.

As the chief crumbled to the ground, keening shrieks of grief and disbelief burst from the confused, milling braves of the gauntlet. Many lie bleeding on the ground, struck down by wild swings of their comrades. Others still clawed at their eyes trying to clean the dirt from them. All began jabbering at once as they wondered how this Lightnin' could have escaped so many powerful warriors.

"Him protected by Great Spirit," grunted one Shawnee.

"No! No!" croaked a wounded Delaware. "Him possessed by demon."

"Not demon!" growled an Ottawa. "Trapper lucky!"

Finally, Bold Wolf leaped forward to rally the savages. He scolded and ranted and shook his hatchet as he enumerated Hawkins' many offenses against them. After noting the gore that oozed from his rent lips, though, only the hot-headed young bucks from his own tribe heeded the chief's eloquent oratory.

A full fifteen minutes went by before Bold Wolf and his small war party charged from the encampment howling with rage and bloodlust. Spotting Jack's plain footprints in the snow, they began to yip like fox hounds on the scent of a fresh quarry. Their excitement soon turned to gasps of wonder when they came upon three sets of tracks where there was only one before.

"Look!" gasped a superstitious brave. "White man split into three beings."

"Him use powerful medicine," agreed another.

"Only trick," countered Bold Wolf, frothing with fury. "Come on! Can't let him get away."

When the chief again sped after Hawkins, only eight braves accompanied him. The others stood gawking at the three sets of footprints and then turned back to their village. Glancing warily about them, they muttered prayers to ward off the evil spirits who had obviously aided the charmed mountain man.

# CHAPTER SEVENTEEN:
# HEAD FOR THE RIVER

Jack glanced behind him just in time to watch the old Delaware chief get blasted off his feet. Then, he raced on until his mouth tasted of copper. He hadn't drunk anything since his capture, and his tongue was swollen and coated with thick mucus. His head pounded from a feverish headache, too, but he dared not stop or think about what ailed him.

Hawkins ran until his legs quivered. Twice he almost fell on his face, and twice more just missed trees that loomed from his blurred peripheral vision. When he was about ready to collapse, Will and Mac miraculously burst from the woods and grabbed him by each arm. Thus steadied, he surged on deliriously for another quarter mile before panting, "Head for the river, boys. I-I-I really need a slug o' water."

The woodsmen veered hard right toward the rushing roar of rapids that echoed through the hemlocks. With his last burst of energy, Jack broke through the undergrowth and stumbled across a narrow beach to the water's edge. There, he fell heavily on all fours like a spent horse and dunked his head in the icy stream.

Hawkins drank his fill and then lay panting in the sand. Finally, he croaked, "Ain't never had a day like this before. Was even worse 'n' the time that rattler nailed me, an' I got powerful sick from its pison. Sure glad ya follered me here."

"Your captors left a trail those Shawnees you blinded could have found," replied Mac. "None of this woulda happened if Will had finished off Bold Wolf when he had the chance."

"When was that?" gasped Lightnin'.

"The day we escaped the fire ring. He knocked that rogue to the ground but didn't have the courage to shoot 'im dead."

"Is that true, Big Cat?"

"I-I-I'm sorry, Jack. I just couldn't kill an unconscious man. . ."

"Wall, he'da sure as heck butchered you!" snarled Lightnin'. "In these here woods only the ruthless sur-vive. Ain't no place fer kindness or indecision."

"I-I-I know that now. I'll never make that mistake again."

"Good! Let's make fer our canoe and git the heck outta here!"

Mac and Will helped Hawkins to his feet and off they stumbled through the snow. They had only gone a short ways upstream when Alex asked, "Are ye sure you didn't get the sense knocked out o' ya, Jack? If we go this way, we'll be right back in the Indians' camp."

"Dang!" whistled Lightnin'. "You're right! Ain't no way we kin fetch our canoe with them in our way."

"What are we going to do, then?" cried Cutler. "Everywhere we go, we leave a wide trail. Maybe we should swim for it."

"Stick your hand in the water, laddie," said Mac. "Ye wouldn't make it halfway to the other bank before your limbs freeze solid."

"Let's git back in the woods, then, where we ain't in plain sight," grunted Hawkins. "Heck! Mebbe we kin find a place to ambush 'em there."

"Aye," agreed Mac. "If we pick off enough o' 'em, we could escape yet."

Just as the mountain men turned to follow Jack's suggestion, two puffs of musket smoke burst from the brush between them and the forest. After both bullets kicked up dirt well in front of them, Lightnin' pointed downstream and howled, "Streak it!"

The trappers pitched along the rocky shore with the whoops of the Ottawas ringing in their ears. The ground was too uneven for them to break into a run, so they dodged and weaved to make harder targets for the Indians who quickly closed within musket range. Soon, bullets were whizzing around them like bees until Will flopped to the ground and drilled the first brave to emerge onto the open river bank.

"Good shot!" exclaimed Lightnin' diving beside him. "Musta been you who ventilated the old chief that was drawin' down on me."

"No, I shot the spear out of the guard's hand."

"An' I killed the knave blockin' the gauntlet," said Mac, kneeling behind a boulder at the water's edge.

"Then who killed the chief?" asked Jack. "He sure didn't shoot hisself."

"We better move again," warned Alexander. "Look! There's two more Ottawas tryin' to get below us."

The woodsmen popped up and bounded down the shoreline until they came to where the riverbank dropped sharply onto a narrow sandbar. Sliding down the incline, they found themselves in a natural fort that shielded them from enemy fire. That didn't stop the Indians, though, from creeping in on three sides until they blocked every lane of escape. After peering over the bank to assess their situation, Will muttered, "It looks like we're trapped, fellas. Now, what do we do?"

"Keep shootin'!" brayed Lightnin', blowing splinters from the hemlock trunk where a nearby Ottawa skulked. "If we kin hold 'em off 'til dark, we'll try an' sneak by 'em."

"That is if we don't run out o' powder first," lamented Alex, shaking his half-empty powder horn.

Now, the Ottawas began to fire in volleys to keep the woodsmen's heads down. While Jack and the others hunkered behind the bank, several braves leaped up to seek cover closer to the desperate trappers. By the fourth volley, two Indians lurked behind boulders only a few leaps away from their enemies' fort.

The fifth barrage had just faded away downriver when the two braves drew their hatchets, and with blood-curdling shrieks, hurdled over the bank. Slashing with their axes, they leaped on Mac and Lightnin' and bowled them over with such force that the trappers lost their long rifles in the melee. Back and forth they tumbled hacking at the squirming mountain men who struggled vainly to pull out their knives.

MacDonald's adversary was much bigger than he, and only the Scot's tenacity kept him in the fight. After receiving a stinging shoulder wound, Mac bit the Ottawa's hatchet hand until he let loose of his weapon. Then, Alex grabbed a big rock and bashed and bashed at the Indian's shaved skull until he quit kicking.

Lightnin' had his hands full, too. His foe whacked him on the side of the head, slicing off a hunk of his scalp. Wailing in pain and anger,

Jack grabbed the Ottawa by the throat and began squeezing until the warrior's eyes bulged unnaturally. The Indian spit in Hawkins' face and then drew his knee up into the woodsman's crotch. Incensed by this new agony, Jack wrestled the hatchet away from his enemy and beat him to death with it.

Will, meanwhile, scrambled to gather all three rifles. Crawling to the top of the bank, he fired deliberately at the Ottawas who continued to inch closer as they listened to the struggles on the sandbar. The Indians were so shifty in their approach that the lad only winged one brave before his guns were empty. He had just begun to hurriedly reload his weapons when Bold Wolf rose from the brush to signal an all-out assault.

Jack and Mac lay clutching their wounds when they heard a crazy cackle echo from upriver. Craning their necks, they saw Bearbite Bob steering his big French canoe through the heart of the rapids directly toward them. Dropping his paddle, he snatched a long rifle from the bottom of his craft and shot so close to Bold Wolf's ear that the Indian was forced to duck back into cover. Grabbing his paddle again, Winslow maneuvered the canoe onto the beach right next to his injured friends.

"Wall, whatcha waitin' fer?" Bob howled. "Git in!"

Will tossed Jack and Mac their rifles and turned to fire one more shot at the Ottawas. Then, he bounded down the bank and dove into the canoe between Hawkins and Alexander. In the next instant, Bearbite pushed off into the river and began a frenzied paddling until the current caught them.

With a disappointed howl, the Indians rushed to the river's edge to fire a parting salvo. Bullets kicked up all around the bobbing craft, while Bearbite cursed every Ottawa who had ever lived with a foul string of expletives that reddened Will's ears. When they whipped downstream and disappeared behind the far side of an island, Cutler finally said, "Thank God you came for us, Bob. How did you know we were here?"

"I been trailin' them red skunks ever since they come an' ruined my trappin'. I even seen 'em take Lightnin'. Weren't nothin' I could do 'bout it at the time, but I figgered he'd escape sooner er later. If he hadn't, I'da rounded up Snakeskin Bill, Black John Innes, an' Killer Miller an' beat them Ottawas at their own scalpin' game. Wagh! There ain't no two Indians can equal a mountain man!"

"Did ya see me run the gauntlet?" cried Jack. "I sure showed 'em a thing er two."

"Jess like me when I drilled that Delaware chief," bragged Bearbite. "I shot 'im from three hundred yards, I did."

"An' I'll bet you be standin' on your head when ye fired that shot," grunted Mac with a pained grimace.

"Sure!" guffawed Bob. "An' I'll be glad to teach ya how I done it once that shoulder o' yers heals up."

# CHAPTER EIGHTEEN:
## SAVING BRIGHT STAR

Bob Winslow expertly guided the canoe through one chute of rapids after another while his exhausted friends slumped in the bottom of the fragile craft. Unfazed by the challenge, he continued to paddle until long shadows stretched across the Allegheny. Finally, just before darkness engulfed them, he steered the canoe onto a black beach.

As Jack, Mac, and Will staggered off into the brush, Bearbite unloaded his heavy backpack and a meager bundle of furs. "That's all the plews I had cached before them Ottawas de-sturbed me," he grumbled. "Dad gum it! One afternoon the stinkin' cusses busted up my camp, stole my traps, an' made off with the last o' my rum. They come while I was out huntin' fer my supper."

"Ye should be thankful ye weren't home at the time," muttered Alex. "We never made it to our trappin' grounds."

"Hey, we's alive, ain't we?" choked Hawkins, collapsing in a patch of ferns. "We got some hard travel ag'in tomorrow. Let's git to snorin'."

"I'm way ahead of you," said Cutler, emitting a deep yawn. "I'm talkin' in my sleep now."

When the woodsmen continued down the river at first light, Will was rested enough to help with the paddling. The Allegheny was much wider here, which made the canoe easier to handle. In the deeper stretches they were able to drift for miles with only a stroke or two to keep their craft going straight.

"Where are we headed?" asked Will nonchalantly as he watched two deer feeding along the far bank. "Logstown?"

"I wish," groaned Bearbite, "but our gals ain't there no more. Snakeskin Bill told me the Frenchies done burned half the village, includin' George Croghan's tradin' house."

"Then, where will we go?" pressed Cutler.

"Down Fort Cumberland way, I reckon. That's the only place on the whole frontier that ain't crawlin' with Indians itchin' fer our scalps."

"We best go ashore, then," said Lightnin' "'cause we's almost floated to the Frenchies' new fort. If we try goin' past all them cannon they got, they'll blow us out o' the water, fer sure."

"Ya mean Fort Duquesne?" replied Bob. "That's what they're callin' her this week, after the governor o' Canada."

With wary glances downriver, the travelers again beached their canoe. After carefully concealing it in the bushes, they sneaked off into the forest along a secret trail known only to Bearbite and a few other mountain men. Mac and Lightnin' still didn't have much endurance and had to rest often. Will, meanwhile, lugged Bob's hefty backpack until he looked as dragged out as his wounded friends.

The woodsmen hadn't traveled south for more than a couple days when a squall whipped through the forest, immersing it in heavy, wet snow. This forced them to take refuge in a rickety cabin they encountered along the path. The wind seeped through the cracks in the log walls and robbed all the heat from the fire they built in the crumbling stone chimney. They huddled together for warmth until the storm finally broke the next morning.

When Bearbite peered out the broken cabin door, he discovered two feet of snow had fallen overnight. Staring back at his wobbly pals, he said, "Mebbe we should winter right here. That'll give you fellers a chance to heal proper. Come outside, Will, an' we'll see if we can't make our lodge a might more comfortable."

Following Bob's lead, Will began packing snow against the walls of the cabin to insulate it from the raw wind. Then, he helped the old trapper cut some five-foot poles that they hammered together with wood pegs. They ripped off the old door and fastened their new one in its place, using strips of rawhide for hinges. They attached the hinges with iron nails Jack found scattered on the dirt floor amid a pile of bones.

Will returned to hunting with his bow now, too, and brought home a steady supply of white-furred, winter rabbits. Bob also taught him how to make snares and deadfall traps that they placed along game trails. Pine needle tea and willow bark completed their meager diet as the snow fell steadily and the wind continued to howl.

Jack and Mac grew stronger with each passing day and by April were completely healed of their wounds. Finally, one fine spring morning, Lightnin' said, "Wall now, I reckon we best be shovin' off fer Will's Creek. Ain't no use bein' fit as a fiddle if I don't rip off a few tunes."

"That's 'xactly what I tell Bear Woman," cackled Bob. "Let's git movin'."

The woodsmen packed their gear and again began creeping deliberately southward. Often, they struggled through ankle-deep mud as they kept to trails only frequented by deer and other forest creatures.   In the remote mountains Hawkins shot a fat buck, and they camped for two days to eat their fill of it.  Refreshed by these hearty meals, they didn't stop again until they trudged onto the narrow streets of Will's Creek.

"So you're back," shouted Thomas Jones from the door of his sprawling log bungalow. "What have ya got to trade this time?"

"Jess one small bundle o' prime plew," lamented Bearbite.

"Don't fret yourself none," answered the trader.  "John Frazer was so happy with the job yer friends done for him last spring that he left you credit to buy anything ya need.  Come on in, and I'll fix ya right up."

"Aye, it pays to be honest," affirmed Mac. "Then, the good Lord takes care o' ya."

Whooping wildly, the trappers charged into the trading post and rifled through Jones' shelves to refit themselves.  Besides the necessary black powder and pigs of lead, they grabbed new hatchets, linen hunting shirts, and heavy wool socks.  When Will added a string of bright beads to the pile, Jones said, "You're a little young to be a squaw man, aren't ya?  But then you must have heard about all them beautiful Iroquois gals camped just this side o' General Braddock's bivouac."

"Braddock?" growled Mac.   "What's that swine doin' here?"

"Why, he's brung a whole army to chase the Frenchies from Fort Duquesne.  There must be a couple thousand British regulars an' Virginia militia over yonder at Fort Cumberland."

"And there's beautiful Indian girls, too?" croaked Will.

"Yes," answered the trader. "The Half-King died last fall, an' Scarouady took his place. This new chief's here to powwow with Braddock. All the powerful Iroquois an' their families come along, too. There's Silver Heels, Great Tree, Captain New Castle, an' Dark Thunder—"

"That's Bright Star's father," interrupted Cutler. "I gotta get cleaned up and go find her."

"Hey! Wait fer me," yelped Bob. "Bear Woman's gotta be there, too."

"Then, we best tag along," chortled Hawkins, "to make sure you fellas don't in-fect the whole British army with that fever that's come over ya. That'd ruin their whole campaign."

The trappers thanked Thomas Jones, snatched up their supplies, and hurried to the well located in the town square. There, Will drew a brimming bucket of ice-cold water and proceeded to wash his hands and face. Then, he stripped off his buckskin shirt and cleansed his torso until he shivered with goose bumps that raised everywhere he splashed himself.

With amusement playing in his brown eyes, Bob watched the lad pull on his new hunting shirt and comb his mane of flax-colored hair. Bearbite, meanwhile, fluttered his fingertips in the icy bucket of water and waved them in the air until they were dry. With a tug on his tangled beard, he snickered, "Wall, that's clean enough fer the gal I go with. I'm ready if you is, Will."

With Cutler and Bearbite well in the lead, the woodsmen bowled along the narrow streets until they came out on a meadow packed with so many tents that it was hard to see the walls of Fort Cumberland in the distance. As the trappers plunged into this sea of canvas, they saw the Virginia flag waving just ahead. When they drew

137

even with the banner, a tall, red-haired officer rose from his camp stool and shouted, "Come over here, gentlemen. We can always use scouts with your experience if you wish to volunteer."

"Our experience?" echoed Alex. "I didn't a think we'd be welcome, Colonel Washington, after leavin' ya on the retreat from Fort Necessity."

"Yes, that was a confusing time," confessed the colonel. "I returned to Mount Vernon soon after that myself. But we all learned from the campaign and can profit from it. How about helping us again, Mac? Will? Hawkins? Your friend is welcome, too."

"Let us think on it," replied Lightnin'. "We sure ain't doin' no trappin' with the woods full o' Ottawas. An' we ain't made fer settin' around neither. We'll come by later with our answer."

"Until then, why don't you visit the British camp and watch them train? Once you've seen their army in action, you can't help but join."

"I've already seen enough o' what the English can do," muttered Mac, "but thank ye anyway, Colonel."

The woodsmen nodded goodbye to Washington and hastened toward a makeshift Indian village built on the fringe of the forest next to the Virginians' camp. Only a few old squaws rested in the shade there, so the trappers gravitated toward the rattling of drums that resounded from the direction of the fort.

As Mac, Will, Bearbite, and Lightnin' drew nearer the drumming, they saw a large crowd of gaping townsfolk and Indians gathered around a well-trampled parade ground. They pushed their way through the mob until they saw stretched before them two full regiments of British regulars dressed in their bright red coats and red pants.

Their polished muskets glistened in the sun as they performed the manual of arms to the crisp bark of officers. After this smart handling of weapons, the soldiers marched and wheeled in exact cadence and then formed into impressive lines of battle without missing a step.

"Wagh!" exclaimed Will. "Those fellows move as one man."

"Aye, on flat, open ground they do," hissed Mac. "But how will they fight in the forest with the brambles a clawin' at their fancy coats?"

"An' them Brown Bess is smoothbores," scoffed Hawkins. "They's meant fer volley firin' an' is only accurate to eighty yards. If their enemy's at two hundred, an' hidin' behind trees an' rocks, they might as well fire at the moon."

"Who are those soldiers on both ends of the line?" jabbered Cutler in wide-eyed admiration. "They gotta be eight feet tall."

"That's the grenadiers," explained Alex. "They're the flank companies an' the cream of the British army. Only the strongest men are chosen for those outfits. O' course their mitre caps make them look taller than they really are."

"I wouldn't give ya a pinch o' sour owl manure fer the whole lot o' them lobster back dandies," sneered Bearbite. "All they make is good targets if ya ask my say in the matter."

"Try tellin' that to them Indian gals," said Jack, pointing toward a bevy of enthralled maidens. "Look at 'em gawk an' giggle."

"Flirt is more like it," grunted Mac. "Why, there's Bright Star and Bear Woman right there in middle o' 'em."

Will's head just about twisted off his neck as he turned to gaze in the direction MacDonald pointed out to him. Before he could spot the

Iroquois princess, a flood of grenadiers dismissed from the ranks swarmed over to the girls and blocked them from view.

"I-I-I gotta get over there," sputtered Cutler, forging ahead through the crowd. "Let's go!"

By the time Will and his friends had wormed their way through the mob, only half the Indian maidens were still where Mac had seen them. The rest strolled hand-in-hand with British soldiers off into the seclusion of the forest. Prominent among them was Bear Woman, who fawned on a strapping grenadier. She smiled repeatedly up into his face as she fingered the laced button holes in the white facing of his uniform. He, in turn, kissed her roughly and then swept her into the brush.

Bright Star was engaged in a different sort of affair. A massive, red-faced soldier had grabbed her by her tiny hand and had begun to pull her against her will toward the woods. "Why you be blowin' me kisses," he bellowed, "if you don't favor my advances?"

"Let her go!" shouted Will, rushing to push the grenadier away. "Don't you know she's a princess?"

"Beat it, runt," growled the big sergeant, knocking Cutler to the ground. "She'll be a queen before I'm done with her."

"Leave her alone," cried Will, bouncing to his feet, "or—"

"Or what, boy? You'll cry until you wet yourself?"

Will swung his small, hard fist with all his might and clocked the big sergeant on the jaw. The grenadier rocked back on his heels and then answered with a powerful roundhouse that hammered his attacker into the growing ring of spectators. Cutler was only down for a second before he blew back out the crowd with fire shooting from his eyes. He tried tackling the stout soldier at the knees but only bounced off his black gaiters. The bully retaliated by viciously kicking Will in the ribs and stomach until the lad rolled madly away from him.

Before Cutler could charge the British soldier again, a redcoat lieutenant surged through the gasping crowd and tried to collar the boy. Mac stuck his rifle stock between the officer's feet, tripping him to the ground. "You'll let 'em fight," hissed Alex to the fallen redcoat, "or feel me Scottish wrath!"

The grenadier had just reached out to grab Bright Star again when Will lowered his head and pawed the ground like an enraged bull. Bolting forward, he hit the soldier in the small of the back, bowling him off his feet. The bully fell with such force that the air surged out of his lungs, rendering him helpless. Cutler then flailed away with his fists drawing blood from the stunned man's lips and nose. He continued to punch his opponent mercilessly until the redcoat pleaded, "Stop! Stop!"

"Who's wetting himself now?" mocked Will. "I won't stop until you apologize to Bright Star."

Cutler kept up his relentless pummeling until the British lieutenant, who Mac had tripped, pulled a whistle from his pocket and blew three sharp blasts from it. In the next instant, a company of grenadiers pushed through the cheering mob to yank the battling boy off their comrade. The officer then rose to his feet and barked, "Help Sergeant Wood to the surgeon, men. And arrest these two ruffians for assaulting his Majesty's soldiers."

"Two ruffians?" asked a bewildered corporal.

"Yes, the boy and this outlaw Scot!" snarled the lieutenant, pointing angrily at MacDonald. "Strip off their shirts! They're about to receive twenty lashes for their insolence."

"How's that fair?" shrieked Will, struggling to escape the soldiers who held him. "It's your man who's the scoundrel here!"

"Add five more lashes to the whelp's punishment," grunted the arrogant officer.

"But all I did was defend the honor of a princess," protested Cutler. "Anyone here can tell you."

"That's exactly right," said George Washington, stepping from the ring of spectators. "Let my men go, Lieutenant."

"Your men?"

"Yes, they're scouts well familiar with the woods we're about to invade. I'll find a suitable punishment for them, and it won't include the cat o' nine tails. These gentlemen are too valuable to our impending campaign to be thus stricken."

"I saw, too," grunted a stern Iroquois chief. "Long knives dishonor the daughters of my people. Not this boy. I stand for it no longer. Come, Bright Star. We go to Ishua Town."

"But, Dark Thunder," sputtered the British officer, "we're counting on our brave Iroquois brothers to defeat the French who build forts on our very doorstep."

"We take our daughters and go," replied the chief furiously. "No more talk."

Will shook off the soldiers who held him to stare longingly at Bright Star. Calling her name, he fumbled feverishly for the beads he had bought for her. In his haste, he yanked so hard on the string that it broke in half just as he pulled it from his pocket. As the flashy baubles spilled on the ground, the lad flushed with embarrassment at his sudden clumsiness.

Luckily the girl's back was toward Will while she obediently joined her father. Then, she turned for a brief moment to share a thankful smile with the lad. Cutler felt the world spin under his feet as he grinned in return and watched her disappear among the crowd. He didn't remember another thing until Lightnin' said next to his ear, "Are you alright, Big Cat? What a thrashin' you give that fella. Them British'll think twice afore tanglin' with you ag'in."

"So we're back in army?" asked Will blankly.

"I reckon so," sighed Hawkins. "Since Washington fetched our fat from the fire, we owe 'im plenty."

"I'll not be a goin'," muttered Mac. "Not after witnessin' more British justice. I'll die before I let any man lay open me back again. That's why I'll stay a free trapper."

"But where will ya trap?" Lightnin' wondered.

"On Iroquois land. I plan to go live with Dark Thunder's people."

"But why would they let ya stay with them?"

"Because I helped Will save their princess. How 'bout you, Bearbite? Do ye want to come with me?"

"No, I best stay with Lightnin' an' Big Cat. Who knows what trouble they'll git theirselves into without me watchin' over 'em?"

"It doesn't have anything to do with Bear Woman, does it?"

"No, Mac. She's a child o' the wind like me an' Hawkins. No one tells us which direction ta blow. Us boys'll come find ya once this campaign's over if any o' us is still standin' by then."

In colonial America, guerilla warfare was favored by the Indians, the French, and the Virginia militia. "One man one tree" was the rule followed by the warriors and soldiers who concealed themselves from their enemies during combat.

# CHAPTER NINETEEN:
# BRADDOCK'S FOLLY

"Boy, we'd have been better off taking those lashes," groaned Will, swinging his heavy ax at a thick oak.

"Yes, this road buildin' turns a fella's arms to rubber," agreed Hawkins, striking the trunk a weak blow.

"I thought we was supposed to be scouts," grumbled Bob. "The only thing I've looked fer in the past month is another tree to hew down."

"So it's scouts you want to be?" growled the nasty grenadier lieutenant, who'd been assigning them all the dirtiest duties since leaving Fort Cumberland. "Then, come with me, and I'll see you get placed in the advance guard."

"The only thing they'll find there is a bullet," sneered Sergeant Wood, the bully that Will had pummeled to save Bright Star. "Maybe in the back."

"Hey, us boys can even find our way in the dark," grunted Lightnin'. "That's why you rousted us out of our blankets at four in the mornin' to blaze this here trail fer yer lumberin' ox of a supply train."

As Will, Jack, and Bob tossed aside their axes, snatched up their long rifles, and followed the officer toward a contingent of soldiers surging through the woods ahead, Cutler muttered, "I thought Washington was going to give us our punishment, not these lobster backs."

"Washington can't help it if he caught the fever an' didn't join Braddock 'til yestiddy," whispered Hawkins.

"What did you say?" growled the lieutenant.

"Uh. . .We was wonderin' who's in charge of this here advanced party," replied Lightnin' slyly.

"Colonel Thomas Gage is who. Be quiet and hurry up."

The grenadier officer hustled the three woodsmen through the forest and just reached Gage's force before it emerged on the north bank of the Monongahela River. There, the lieutenant approached the British commander and said, "Colonel, sir, I have three provincials who would like to join your scouting party."

"And welcome they are," rumbled Gage. "The only other skirmishers we have today are George Croghan and seven Mingo."

"Then, we's yer men!" exclaimed Winslow with a lopsided salute. "Bearbite Bob, Lightnin' Hawkins, an' Big Cat Cutler at yer service, sir."

"Alright, go forward with the others," ordered the colonel. "We're only ten miles from Fort Duquesne, so keep a sharp eye."

The mountain men cut around the three hundred regulars and took up their position in the thin line of scouts fanned out in front of the redcoats. They splashed through the low waters of the Monongahela and led the way along the open plain that followed the south bank. The sun shone brightly into the river, making it shimmer emerald green. "Look at the color o' the water," whistled Hawkins. "That should warm the cockles o' yer Irish heart, eh Croghan?"

"Indeed it do," replied the big trader with a grin. "Now, if I only had a wee bit o' sippin' whiskey to soothe me throat, I'd sing ye a few bars of 'Mary Do You Fancy Me'."

When the scouts reached the ford to the north bank, they wheeled and again crossed the river. There, they spotted the burnt ruins of a familiar dwelling that caused Lightnin' to groan, "Poor John Frazer. Them Frenchies dog him wherever he goes. Look at what they done to his new tradin' post."

"And after he was so kind to us, too," lamented Will.

Beyond Frazer's, the woods opened up more than Hawkins remembered. Then, he saw how Indian hunters had burned the underbrush in a series of recent ring hunts. The land here began to slowly rise toward two succeeding pieces of high ground. To the right Jack observed a low forested hill. To the left he saw a series of timber-choked ravines that made him sweat.

"This ain't where I'd choose to fight," Jack whispered to Bearbite as he glanced nervously about.

"Me neither! I'da stuck closer to the river."

When Gage's advance force had reached the top of the first high ground, Hawkins turned and stared at the vast British army stretched out for over a mile behind him. Just a short way down the slope tramped a weary company of road builders followed by a creaking line of wagons that carted the workmen's tools and supplies. Next, came a detachment of horse soldiers followed by Braddock's heavy cannon. Behind the artillery was the main body of redcoats. Fanned out on either side of another long line of wagons, the soldiers stepped lively to the "Grenadiers' March" played by the fife men and drummers. Their regimental flags flapped proudly in the breeze, and their polished muskets glinted in the bright summer sun. Blinded by this glare, Jack squinted a long time before spotting the rear guard marching near the ruins of Frazer's place.

Seeing a large clump of blue-coated Virginia militia at the end of the last column, Lightnin' asked, "Why would Braddock stick his best Indian fighters way back there?"

"Because he looks down his nose at all us colonials," muttered Cutler. "I still can't figure out why Washington agreed to be one of his aides."

"Hey, enough o' that talk," scolded Winslow. "We best keep our eyes peeled fer Frenchies."

The scouts had just worked their way to the top of the second highland when Hawkins froze and pointed into the woods ahead. "Wagh!" he shouted. "There they are!"

Directly in front of the British advance guard appeared a large force of French regulars, Canadian bush rangers, and Ottawa Indians. In the lead was a young officer in a buckskin hunting shirt. Jack knew he was in charge from the silver gorget flashing around his neck. Waving his wide-brimmed hat in the air, the Frenchman howled, "Vive le Roi," and then ordered his men to fire.

Hawkins judged the enemy to be a good two hundreds distant by the way most of their musket volley fell well short of the British ranks. Flopping on his belly, Jack raised his long rifle and drew a bead on the animated fellow waving his hat. Just as he touched off a shot, Gage's men behind him cut loose with a thunderous volley. When the smoke cleared, the French leader lay piled up in a heap along with a few of his comrades that Lightnin' guessed had been felled by the other scouts lying prone beside him.

The British furiously loaded their pieces and fired another salvo at the wavering enemy. In the next instant, Braddock's battery was brought to bear and roared with thunderous fire. Although the cannon rounds were wide of their mark, the noise created by the big guns caused the Indians to scatter.

Jack could see another French officer madly flourishing his sword to rally his countrymen. As the captain got them to stand their ground, the Indians peeled off into the woods and began circling around both flanks of the redcoats. Many sought places of ambush in the wooded ravines, while the others took up positions on the hill above the British column. Jack took a couple shots at the streaking Ottawas, but both bullets were deflected by the brush.

Once the Indians reached cover, they showered the British with unceasing fire and blood-curdling wolf howls. Their crazed war whoops unnerved the British veterans, and Jack saw the grenadiers' resolve begin to crumble as they started a slow retreat toward the wagons behind them. Twice, Colonel Gage ordered his men to fix bayonets and charge up the hill to dislodge the Ottawas there. Despite his entreaties, the British would not quit the line of march. Packed together in tight formation, they made easy targets for the Indians on the high ground, causing Hawkins to remember Bold Wolf's promise to pick off his foes like one pigeon.

The British began firing wildly into the woods wherever puffs of musket smoke appeared. Not bothering to identify their mark, they soon began mowing down their own flank companies and several Virginia units that had rushed into the forest to root out the lurking Indians. At the peak of this confusion, Will shouted, "What do we do? We'll be killed if we stay here."

"To the wagons, boys!" yelped Hawkins. "That's the only safe place on this battlefield."

Jack, Will, and Bob slithered on their bellies down the hill. After squirming under the road builders' supply train, they scanned the hill above for someone to shoot at. There was now so much smoke swirling in the heights that they were forced to hold their fire.

"We's in the pickle brine up to our noses," gulped Winslow. "If we stand with the English, the Ottawas'll blast us. If we go lookin' fer the savages, the redcoats'll shoot us in the back."

"Pinned down is what they call it," grunted Hawkins. "We'll jess have to stay hid an' hope the Indians charge so we kin git a clean shot at 'em."

By then, what remained of the advance unit had fallen back to the line of wagons in a tangled mob. At that exact moment Jack saw the main British force stream forward to enter the fray. These redcoats immediately became tangled with those who had retreated in disorder, making it even easier for the Ottawas to snipe them. Adding to the chaos, the French turned around some captured cannon and began lobbing round shot into the head of the British column.

"I ain't heared so much hellfire this side o' a Jonathan Edwards' sermon," cried Bearbite after exploding cannon balls had showered them with dirt. "'Sinners in the Hands of an Angry God' be his message."

"I didn't think you were religious," bleated Will.

150

"I ain't. I only went to his church to get out o' the rain."

"I wish that church was close-by now," said Hawkins, "an' that it had walls thick enough to de-flect them round shot."

When all appeared lost, General Braddock rode into the midst of the bedlam with Colonel Washington at his side. The general screamed out orders and waved his sword to punctuate each command. Soon, he had his men back in rank and firing volleys into the woods on three sides. As Hawkins watched, Braddock had four horses shot out from under him. After he mounted his fifth steed, Jack exclaimed, "I thought the general was too short, fat, an' old to be much o' a fighter. Wagh! Was I wrong!"

"Wall, they don't call 'im 'Bulldog' fer nothin'," replied Bob.

"And look at Colonel Washington!" bawled Cutler. "He seems to be everywhere at once. There he goes again."

As the woodsmen gaped in awe, the colonel galloped across the open ground to deliver orders for General Braddock. Several times they saw him rock in the saddle as bullets ripped through the baggy sleeves of his coat. Ignoring the proximity of the musket fire, he continued to speed back and forth until his horse's neck dissolved in a bloody spray.

"Dang!" yelped Will. "The colonel's in trouble. We better go help him."

"You're right," agreed Lightnin', crawling out from under the wagon. "Let's streak it!"

Cutler, Winslow, and Hawkins raced toward Washington as he struggled to free himself from his downed steed. They yanked feverishly on the groaning beast's neck until George pried free his leg. Leaping up, the colonel then led the woodsmen to help a cannon crew helplessly frozen by fear. At George's direction, Will and Jack loaded the field piece and wheeled it into position. With his own hands, the intrepid officer then discharged the gun into a pocket of Indians concealed in a nearby ravine.

"That'll teach them skunks!" howled Bearbite when he saw several Ottawas blown skyward. "Way to shoot!"

With Bob's huzzahs still ringing in his ears, Washington jumped on the back of another horse and charged off to rally a group of stragglers. He had just gotten the Virginians into battle formation when Indians skulking in some nearby rocks unleashed a fearsome barrage. Seeing the carnage caused by this salvo, the colonel suddenly wheeled his mount and galloped off to consult with General Braddock.

Jack and his comrades tore along behind Washington and just reached his side when they heard the colonel plead, "General, our men are being mercilessly cut down here in the open. Wouldn't it be wise to get them into cover of the trees?"

"Into cover?" blustered Braddock. "Why, that's downright cowardice! Keep the men formed up, I say. And fire in volleys! I command the finest fighting men in the world. They still shall win the day against these undisciplined savages."

"Yes, sir."

Brandishing their rifles, Jack, Bob, and Will formed a protective ring around Washington as bullets whined past the charmed officer. The British commanders weren't so lucky, for the Ottawas began shooting anyone on horseback. Soon, Hawkins saw that Colonel Gage, Colonel

Burton, Sir John St. Clair, and Sir Peter Halket were all absent from their saddles. The terrible whoops echoed louder each time a rider fell to Indian fire. Taking advantage of the evening shadows, the enemy crept closer to make their aim even more deadly.

Braddock, meanwhile, descended to the ground to drive some skulking redcoats out from under a nearby wagon with the flat of his sword. He had just remounted his horse when Lightnin' heard a terrible thwack. Turning at the sound, he saw the general clutch his right arm and slump forward in the saddle. Immediately, some nearby grenadiers dropped their muskets and ran pell-mell toward the river ford behind them. Soon, the whole hillside was alive with sprinting redcoats who ignored Washington's vigorous attempts to rally them.

"Might as well try stopping wild bears," the colonel lamented before ordering Captain Stewart of the Virginia Light Horse to assist General Braddock from the field.

"I'll help him," replied Stewart, "but you should come, too."

When Washington reluctantly galloped off the battlefield, Hawkins, Winslow, and Cutler also took to their heels. As they streaked for the safety of the river ford, every ravine and hillside around them vomited howling Ottawas. With hideous shrieks, the Indians rushed forward to scalp and plunder the dead, totally ignoring the escaping woodsmen.

Will watched this spectacle of horror unfold while attempting to keep pace with his racing friends. With perverse fascination he marked the gory ritual of red devils hacking the hair from the fallen. He also saw them round up twelve terrified grenadiers whom they stripped naked. The soldiers quivered and shook and pleaded for mercy but instead were clubbed and prodded by the savages dancing jubilantly around them. When Will saw that Bright Star's molester was among the captured, he couldn't help but feel sympathy for him.

Cutler continued to run until his temples pounded from the exertion. No matter how fast he pumped his legs, he couldn't stay even with Bearbite and Lightnin'. As he chugged alone down the slope, he heard the thundering of horse's hooves behind him. Wheeling just in time, he saw a ruddy-faced frontiersman astride a draft horse bearing down on him. The frantic rider had lost his hat, and his black hair flapped in the breeze. "Git outta the way," he bellowed, "or Dani'l Boone will run ya over!"

At the last instant Will dove off the path and rolled wildly to keep from being trampled. As he dusted himself off, he saw the horse's cut traces streaming behind it. When Boone never turned to see if Will was okay, the lad shouted, "Watch it, wagon driver! At least you coulda unhitched your team before scampering!"

Cutler crawled to his feet and broke into a painful lope. While he jogged down the incline leading to the Monongahela, he glanced to his left toward a deep gully swirling with musket smoke. It was then that a shrieking warrior leaped from the haze, waving a deadly hatchet. The fiend's face and torso were painted a hideous black, and he raised a blood-curdling wolf howl when he spied three wounded redcoats crawling desperately for the river. The Ottawa dashed forward to hack at each soldier with animal frenzy. It wasn't until the savage waved their dripping scalps victoriously above his head that Will saw the distinct wolf claw necklace adorning the red man's throat.

Will skidded to a halt, threw his long rifle to his shoulder, and drew a steady bead on Bold Wolf's chest. The Indian was too busy celebrating his gore-soaked trophies to duck or run. Cutler continued to squeeze the trigger until his gun misfired with a loud click. Alerted by the snap of the hammer, Bold Wolf glared toward Will and then fixed him with a soul-freezing sneer. In the next instant he vanished in the smoke as the lad blinked back tears of frustration and shame.

# CHAPTER TWENTY: WILL THE WARRIOR

"We're terrible soldiers, aren't we?" snuffed Will when he found his friends waiting for him on the other side of the river.

"A mountain man's first duty ain't to no king. It's to survive. Don't talk. Run!" yipped Lightnin', again breaking into a sprint.

"Hoof it!" cried Bearbite. "Savin' your topknot is all that's important now."

The three woodsmen raced along the south bank of the Monongahela until they saw a company of wounded redcoats staggering along just ahead. The British had thrown away their weapons and looked more like a herd of sheep than proud grenadiers. The abased soldiers never even looked up when Jack shouted, "Hurry, men! You kin still save yerselves."

Dashing past the limping fugitives, Hawkins and his buddies encountered a small body of dazed Virginia militia next. "We's all that's left," mourned a short private, gesturing to his thirty comrades. "We took three companies into battle, an' look how they got slaughtered."

"An' mostly by the unnerved English," growled a second bluecoat.

Jack, Will, and Bob continued to run until they spotted an armed detachment commanded by the bleeding Colonel Burton. "Don't shoot! Don't shoot!" they howled before rushing on through the British ranks.

The mountain men collapsed panting to the ground. When they had finally caught their breath, they saw General Braddock lying beneath a tree surrounded by George Washington, Dr. Craik, and several British officers. The doctor was dressing Braddock's wounds, and a concerned frown passed over his face when he saw how weak the general had become.

After many minutes, Braddock raised his head and whispered, "Colonel Washington. . .I want you to go Dunbar's Camp. . .Bring back wagons for the wounded. . .We'll stage a holding action. . .Here."

"Yes, sir!"

As Washington galloped away with an escort of soldiers, many other British fled into the woods. This forced Burton to retreat with his remaining troops across the second ford. While Hawkins, Bearbite, and Will splashed through the river, Jack murmured, "Where's all the fifes an' drums now? There can't be more 'n' a hundred fellas making this here stand."

Burton's little army continued to fall back until they reached the place they camped the night before the battle. There, a wounded Colonel Gage limped from the woods leading a small band of troops he had rallied. Hawkins saw the two officers exchange hurried whispers and then order their men to retreat yet again.

When darkness began spreading through the forest, Jack signaled to his pals, and they faded into the shadows. After the British had clattered away, Hawkins said, "I reckon them Ottawas are too busy celebratin' their vict'ry to stick around here. Let's head back to Fort Duquesne an' see what they's up to."

"Shouldn't we just leave?" gulped Will. "There's no use risking our necks again."

"I'm with Lightnin'," grunted Bearbite. "I've always be the curious sort, anyhow, an' I've been hankerin' to use this here telescope I found layin' next to a dead redcoat. A few gold sovereigns mighta fell out o' his pocket, too, but that's 'tween you an' me an' the Monongahela."

"Then, let's go!" exclaimed Jack.

Using the stars as their guide, the three woodsmen crept back to the battlefield. All around them lay mutilated corpses, many stripped of their uniforms, weapons, and belongings. The wagons, too, had been emptied, and the captured cannons dragged away. The July heat had done its work, as well, causing a great stench to rise from the ghastly scene. The trappers quickened their pace to escape it, gagging as they hit the trail to the French fort.

Hawkins and his friends arrived at the Forks of the Allegheny at sunrise. Creeping cautiously on their bellies, they wormed to the edge of the forest to employ Bearbite's spyglass. Decked out in red jackets and military hats, the Indians still howled and danced about the gates of the fort. Many Ottawas, drunk on blood, brandished their tomahawks or waved handfuls of scalps in the air. Smoking fires were evidence that the celebration had lasted all night.

Suddenly, a volley of shots burst from the mob of jubilant Indians. With a fresh chorus of shrieks, the savages dragged twelve British prisoners from the fort. The soldiers had been stripped naked and had their faces painted a grim black. They didn't even struggle when led to a line of stakes driven into the river bank.

When Will saw what was about to happen, he passed the telescope to Jack and closed his eyes. Hawkins gasped as he watched the soldiers' torture unfold. Each prisoner in turn was tied to a stake with his hands above his head. Some of the Ottawas probed their victim with hot irons. Others stuck burning pine splinters in the squirming man's flesh to set him on fire. Each wail of agony caused the savages to dance madly and howl with sadistic delight. To enjoy the gruesome entertainment longer, the Indians only roasted one man at a time.

"How can the French let this happen?" sobbed Will when the shrieks reached a fever pitch.

"They're givin' the devils their due," replied Lightnin' after handing Bearbite the telescope.

"I seen enough," grunted Bob. "Let's go."

The mountain men crawled carefully back into the woods, rose to their feet, and slipped off to the north. When they had gone a short way, Cutler asked, "Where are we going now?"

"To Ishua Town to find Mac," murmured Hawkins. "This whole frontier's gonna go up in smoke once news o' the Frenchies' victory reaches the Delawares an' Shawnees. You can bet yer topknot on it."

"Them tribe's been perchin' on the fence to see which side's gonna win," agreed Bob. "Mebbe we best walk a little faster."

The woodsmen picked up their pace as the scorching sun rose above the horizon. They continued to hurry along until Lightnin' came to a sudden halt and eeked back the hammer of his flintlock. Motioning into the hemlock on both sides of the trail, he raised his gun and took two more cautious steps.

Will and Bearbite also cocked their pieces and peered into the thick woods around them. Cutler, who was slightly behind his friends, felt his flesh prickle with anticipation. Horrific scenes of wailing, scalped soldiers panned through his brain until his legs began to quiver beneath him. Adding to his alarm were three quick caws that shattered the forest silence. It was then that he whirled to peer down the trail in back of him.

Just as he turned, a hatchet sliced through the air inches from his head. Before he could recover from his surprise, Bold Wolf howled balefully and struck another blow that neatly severed Will's possibles bag from his shoulder. The woods now rang with hideous whoops, and Cutler swung his rifle to blast another Ottawa that leaped at him from the side of the trail. He heard two more musket reports behind him as he again juked away from Bold Wolf's flailing ax.

Throwing down his empty gun, Will jerked a tomahawk out of his belt and slashed wildly at his enemy. Bold Wolf danced out of the way of the lad's flurry of swings and then mocked him with a flurry of his own aimed at nothing. Reddening at the insult, the lad swung twelve more times at the dodging chief. Bold Wolf's smile widened with each unsuccessful attack as he watched his enemy tire. Then, he delivered a precise blow that neatly severed the head from Will's hatchet handle.

Will tossed the handle aside and reached to draw his knife. As the lad plucked it from its sheath, Bold Wolf rushed forward to plant his tomahawk in Will's right shoulder. Cutler cried out in pain and thrust his weapon with all his might. The blade sliced through sinewy muscle, leaving a trail of blood across the chief's ribcage.

Bold Wolf yelped, wrenched free his hatchet, and leaped away. Before he charged Will again, the young mountain man flung his knife with a powerful, fluid motion. The blade penetrated the chief's throat, knocking him backward over a log. The Ottawa gurgled, gasped, and then collapsed, brushing at the black gore pouring down the front of his chest.

Will snatched up his long rifle and desperately reloaded it. As he poured priming powder into the pan, he saw two more Ottawas running pell-mell up the path toward him. Yanking his gun to his wounded shoulder, he aimed for the neck of the lead warrior. He felt an excruciating pain rock him with the concussion of the rifle. Wincing, he watched his patched ball blow a cloud of bloody spray from the first brave. To Will's surprise, the second Ottawa fell, too, as the bullet continued on its deadly course to strike him through the chest.

Flailing his rifle like a club, Cutler whirled to face a sudden commotion coming from behind him. There, he saw Lightnin' locked in a death struggle with Deep Waters, the Shawnee chief. The Indian had Hawkins pinned to the ground and was trying to force his knife into the trapper's chest. Jack used both hands to push away the weapon and then drew his knee repeatedly up into the chief's crotch. Deep Waters grunted and relaxed his grip on the knife. When it slipped from his grasp, Lightnin' smashed him in the ear with a mighty blow of his fist. Then, he whipped a hatchet from his belt and added a second scar to the chief's face. Deep Waters shrieked once and toppled over dead.

Will was about to yell his congratulations when another disturbance washed over him. Turning at the repeated thuds, he saw Bearbite smashing a Delaware to the ground with the stock of his rifle. He hit the brave repeatedly on the head, driving him downward as if he were a tent peg. When the Indian finally sprawled over on his back, a huge gash had opened in his skull and both of his eyes were swollen shut. Bob then drew his hatchet and whacked the Delaware until he quit moving.

The mountain men converged in the middle of the path and stood together with their backs touching. Facing three different directions, they scanned the brush for another wave of attackers. When they found themselves alone with the Indians they had killed, Winslow said, "Let's git to scalpin' these heathens, boys."

"What do you mean s-s-scalping?" stammered Will.

"Hey, ya wanna show the Iroquois you're a mighty warrior, don't ya?"

"Couldn't I just take Bold Wolf's necklace?"

"Bold Wolf?" echoed Hawkins. "So that's the rascal who stirred up these Shawnees an' Delawares. No wonder I didn't spy him at the fort torturin' them poor British fellas."

"I think his name should be 'Buzzard Wolf'," growled Cutler. "I saw him after the battle yesterday preying on the wounded. I'da killed him then if my gun hadn't misfired."

"Aye, he was always skulkin' 'round the woods lookin' fer some trapper to ambush. I never did see 'im leadin' no charge or facin' an enemy, proper like," agreed Bob.

"If I hadn't remembered you telling me to watch my back, I'd have ended up just like my father with the Wolf's hatchet sticking from the back of my head," croaked Will. "Thanks, Bearbite."

"Anytime, Big Cat. Let's get to scalpin'."

"I still don't see why we should act like those savages," muttered Will.

"All the tribes consider scalps big medicine," assured Hawkins. "It's their way o' showin' their power an' bravery. A scalp's visible proof o' yer kill. That way ya can't lie 'bout what ya done in battle."

"H-H-How do you take a scalp, then?"

"Well, Big Cat," replied Bob, "it's easy as peelin' the white stripes off any skunk's back. In a man's case, ya lift the hair from the crown o' his head. That's easy with an Indian, 'cause that's the only place he grows any hair."

"Hey, Will, ya still got that mountain lion skin?" asked Hawkins. "If so, we need to make ya a cap with the lion's face on it. That'll impress the heck out o' them Iroquois, too."

"Remember? I sold the skin at Fort Cumberland. But I still got the dressed head in my possibles bag," said Will, wincing with pain.

"Hey, the lad's hurt!" exclaimed Bearbite.

"It's nothin'," mumbled Cutler, clutching his shoulder. "Buzzard Wolf nicked me with his hatchet is all."

"Whacked you is more like it!" gasped Jack after he examined the deep wound.

"Hey, we'll boil wintergreen an' wax together an' make 'im some salve," said Bob. "He'll be fine as frog's fur in no time. That's jess a little scratch to a brave. Ain't that right, Big Cat?"

"Yes, sir!" proclaimed Will with a wide grin. "I guess I proved myself today, after all. Now, I'll be all set if you'll teach me what to say to the Iroquois to convince them I'm a great warrior."

# CHAPTER TWENTY-ONE: ISHUA TOWN

It took Lightnin', Bearbite, and Big Cat a month of cautious travel to reach Ishua Town on the upper Allegheny. One fine summer morning they strode toward the palisade gates of the village, casting long shadows before them. After brazenly saluting the guards, they filled the air with scalp halloos and a flurry of shots from their long rifles.

As the startled Iroquois spilled from their longhouses to surround the interlopers, Will waved four scalps above his distinctive lion hat and growled, "I'm Big Cat Cutler. I'm here to see Dark Thunder and proclaim my love for his daughter. I've returned from a great victory over the Iroquois' hated foes, the Ottawas, and have slain their powerful chief, Bold Wolf. See. Here is his scalp and necklace, which I wish to give Dark Thunder to show my esteem for him."

The crowd parted to allow the Iroquois sachem to examine Cutler's war trophies. After a moment, the chief proclaimed, "It is as this brave says. Bold Wolf is no more. As for Bright Star, you must speak to her mother. It is Iroquois law. I, though, accept your gifts."

Jabbering excitedly, the mob pressed forward to touch the scalps and pat Cutler with respectful hands. As Will basked in his new-found acclaim, he saw Bright Star peeking out of the door of her dwelling at him. When she spotted him looking back, she coyly ducked inside the longhouse and drew a deerskin curtain over the opening.

A moment later the curtain parted again and out stepped Alexander MacDonald with a big grin splitting his face. He rushed to shake hands with Will, Jack, and Bob and then shouted, "Welcome, lads, I be worried about ya since word of Braddock's defeat reached here by runner two weeks ago. I'm glad the redcoats got what was a comin' to 'em for their cruelty an' arrogance. I'm even happier to see your faces."

"So you're stayin' with Bear Woman's clan, are ya?" asked Bob. "How is the old gal?"

"Sorry as a trapped beaver. She's a waitin' inside if ye wish to see her."

"Wish to see her? Wall now, ain't that rich! I wanna do a lot more 'n' that. I'll catch up to you fellers later. Much later!"

As Bearbite rushed inside the Bear clan longhouse, Mac slapped Cutler on the shoulder and blabbed, "I've had a chance to talk to Bright Star for you, Will. She was impressed by how you defended her at Fort Cumberland. I heard her whispering to her friends about how handsome ye be, too."

When MacDonald saw Will wince, the Scot added, "Did I do somethin' wrong? I thought ye just told the whole village ya liked her. Ye bellowed it loud enough for me to hear ye inside."

"No! No!" brayed Hawkins. "He likes her fine. You jess touched his tender shoulder. Bold Wolf whacked 'im with his hatchet there."

"I'm sure glad ye ended that villain's life," said Alex wryly. "Now, maybe me red hair will a keep growin' where the good Lord intended it to."

"Enough o' this talk," interrupted Lightnin'. "If ya know Bright Star so good, Mac, why don't ya intraduce our young friend to her before he has a fit o' apoplexy."

With a chuckle MacDonald opened the longhouse curtain and motioned Will inside. Moving through the smoky interior, he led the lad past a row of sleeping platforms to a distant compartment where a lithe girl bent over a stone hearth cooking breakfast. When Mac and Will approached her, she stood shyly and looked down at her fancy, beaded moccasins.

"Bright Star," said Mac with a disarming grin, "I'd like ye to meet Will Cutler. He's a fine young gentleman and brave, too. But I think ye know that already. He'd like to talk to you if you're willin'."

"You hungry?" asked the girl. "We eat before talk."

The girl motioned for the men to be seated on a bear skin spread on the floor. MacDonald, however, tiptoed away while Cutler sat cross-legged waiting to be fed. As Bright Star handed Will a steaming bowl of stew, her mother, Sparrow, entered the compartment and fixed the lad with a hostile stare. Eating her breakfast in cold silence, the woman glowered at him from across the room like he was a thieving coon that had barged into the longhouse. Concealing his fear and anticipation, Will nodded to her gravely and gobbled his food with obvious relish. Finally, the squaw picked up an empty water pot and shuffled away without speaking once to Cutler.

When Sparrow had gone, Will murmured, "That was mighty fine venison stew you cooked, Bright Star. I really enjoyed it."

"Mother make, not me," replied the girl, again glancing at her moccasins.

"You shouldn't look down so much. Your blue eyes are too pretty to hide like that."

Bright Star suppressed a little smile and then snapped, "All you English flatter. You are no different than the others."

"Yes, I am," objected Will, his face turning red beneath his tan. "I would never hurt you like they wanted to. I-I-I think you are the most precious woman God ever created."

"So now you mock the Great Spirit? How can I trust a man who tells such lies?"

"Look in my eyes, and you'll see what I say is true," said Will, rising to face the pretty girl.

"No!"

"But we have too much in common not to be friends. Your reddish hair tells me you weren't born an Indian. That means both of us were captured."

"More lies!" stormed the maiden.

"No, I was taken by Bold Wolf's people after he killed my father. But I escaped."

"Dark Thunder is my father. Sparrow my mother. I not remember other parents. I am happy to be one of the real human beings."

"And I would be happy to live here, too," choked Will, "if you'll have me. Being with you is all that matters."

"I do not believe you."

"Then, believe this. I grew up in a house with six sisters and know how to respect women. I miss having girls around to share my feelings with. I only wish you could do that for me."

"Then why not go back to sisters?"

"They live across the big water in England where the king makes everyone sad. I love living free in these woods. I'd love it even more if I could be with you."

Bright Star considered Will's words for a moment and then motioned toward the door. "You come back tonight," she commanded. "Storyteller be here. We listen. Talk."

"I'll see you then," choked Cutler, reaching out to touch the girl's hand.

As the lad's fingers brushed Bright Star's, he felt a charge of electric shoot half-way up his arm. She must have felt it, too, for her stern look softened and she repeated, "Come back tonight, Will."

"Sure. . ."

Quivering with emotion, Will stumbled away through the murky longhouse. Often, he turned to glance back at the Indian princess. This caused him to bang into roof posts, compartment doorways, and a multitude of clay pots. He made so much racket that Bob growled at him from behind the drawn curtain of Bear Woman's sleeping platform, "Dad burn it! How's a feller to get any lovin' with all that noise?"

"Sorry, Bearbite," sputtered Cutler. "I-I-I was just leaving."

Will staggered out into the bright sunlight and rejoined Mac and Jack, who sat together near the longhouse entrance with their backs against the wall. The lad collapsed beside them with a stunned look on his face, causing Alexander to ask, "What happened to you in there? Ye look like ye were hit by lightnin'."

"Wall now, that ain't possible," joshed Hawkins, "'cause I've been settin' right here the whole time. If I'da smacked Big Cat, he'd be landin' at Fort Cumberland 'bout now."

Cutler smiled weakly at the joke and then lapsed into a dazed silence that lasted the whole afternoon. Twice, he refused cornbread brought to him by some kindly squaws and twice more declined drinks of cold water. Finally, about sundown, he saw a heavily tattooed elder enter the village chanting a singsong prayer. Breaking into a snaky dance, the elder weaved his way through the gathering crowd. By the time he ducked past Will into the Bear clan longhouse, a host of children followed in his wake.

Cutler guessed this must be the storyteller Bright Star told him of, so he rose and entered to find the young maiden. Jack and Mac had long ago dozed off in contented naps, and their long snores followed the lad through the entrance. Peering past the blaze of the central hearth, he finally spotted the princess curled up on a sleeping platform. The next instant she waved to him, and he pushed his way through the chattering crowd of children to cuddle next to her.

The storyteller lifted a clay pipe to his lips and puffed on it until he filled the compartment with blue tobacco smoke. Snatching a turkey feather fan from beneath his robe, he gestured dramatically and began speaking in solemn tones. This hushed the crowd, and the enthralled children listened intently with round, bulging eyes so as not to miss a word or movement.

Suddenly, the storyteller twisted up his cheeks, accenting the green hues etched in his skin. Laughing wickedly, he bent his body one way and then the other. Afterward, he wiggled his fingers above his head and broke into another fiendish cackle that caused the children to scream and cover their faces.

When Will had recovered from his surprise, he whispered to Bright Star, "What was all that about? He just scared the heck out of me."

"Him tell tale of Atotaroh, the Onondaga who so twisted with evil, snakes grew from his hair. Listen. He start again."

The storyteller began to sing and chant to slow his convulsions. Finally, he sat stone still and closed his eyes. He waved his fingers, and a comb magically appeared in his tattooed hand. He ran the comb methodically through his hair as he renewed his chant. When he opened his eyes again, they were clear and bright. He then addressed the applauding children with a short monologue and held up the comb for all to see. On it Will recognized the dual faces of good and evil. This caused him to ask, "Who changed Atotaroh to a peaceable man? Was it the Great Spirit that combed the snakes from his hair?"

"No," replied Bright Star. "It was Hiawatha. Him enchant the evil one with the Hymn of Peace. Him cure Atotaroh so he use his evil for good and become head of Five Nations."

"Wagh!" exclaimed Will. "That sounds like a story Lightnin' would tell. Only he'd have been the hero."

"But this tale true," insisted the girl. "You not believe?"

"I do if you do," said Cutler with a soft smile. "I-I-I want to learn all the Iroquois legends if you'll teach them to me."

Will took Bright Star's small, soft hand in his. He looked deep in her responding eyes until his heart beat so fast it made him dizzy. He wanted to kiss her in the worst way until he saw Sparrow lurking in the shadows watching him.

# CHAPTER TWENTY-TWO:
## WILL'S WEDDING

Will snared the deerskin ball in the webbing of his hickory lacrosse stick and flew upfield with it. Several athletic Seneca youth rushed to cut him off as he raced toward their team's door. He dodged one player and outran a second. The third, though, was quicker than Cutler and cut him off just before he got into position to fling the ball past the door guard and into the goal. The Seneca, with long hair flying, struck Will's stick with his own, causing the ball to squirt loose. Luckily, it rolled directly to Alexander MacDonald, who snared it with one practiced motion and then hurled it with all his might.

When the ball zipped past the door guard before he could react, Mac raised a victorious halloo and rushed to embrace his teammate. He and Cutler danced and yelled as the rest of their squad of Mohawks joined the celebration. While they trooped off the field, Will shouted, "Boy, am I glad I came with you today, Alex, instead of going hunting with Dark Thunder, Lightnin', and Bearbite. Teh hon tsi kwaks eks is really fun."

"Aye, laddie, I've been playin' lacrosse ever since I come here to keep me in proper shape."

"Bright Star calls it the Creator's game. She says it's played for the Creator's enjoyment and to restore harmony to the people."

"It's also good practice for war," added MacDonald. "The Iroquois didn't subdue their Indian enemies by accident, ye know."

"It's a good time, anyway you look at it."

"How's things goin' with you an' Sparrow? She's the one ye must beat to win the game you're playin'."

"She should be named Sparrow Hawk," grumbled Will. "I swear her beady eyes are on me every time I try to be alone with Bright Star."

"Well, ye've only been here a month now. The way ye've gotten along with everyone else in the village, I'd say it's only a matter of time before she accepts you, too."

"I'm doing everything I can to please her. I can't even count the number of fat deer I've brought to her door. That's also why I insisted we play with the visiting Mohawks today. That was Sparrow's tribe before Dark Thunder married her."

"At least she hasn't run ye off," chuckled Mac. "That in itself be a good sign."

"Hey, is that screaming I hear?" barked Cutler, cocking his ear to the wind. "It's coming from the direction of town. Let's hoof it!"

Brandishing their lacrosse sticks like weapons, Will and Mac raced back to Ishua Town with the last bit of spring left in their legs. Rushing through the gate, they saw a train of strange pack horses strung out in front of the town dwellings. Two grimy men with four days' pig stubble on their faces were there, too. They were trading rum to the elated braves over the protests of their wives. The squaws raised a fearful din and beat at the traders with their tiny, closed fists. The barrel-chested scoundrels brushed off the women as though they were gnats as greed burned in their eyes and tobacco juice drooled from the corners of their sneering lips.

When two Senecas tried swapping their precious hunting rifles, Will saw Sparrow leap in front of them and strike the stockiest trader across the face with a willow switch before he could collect the guns. Howling with fury, the ruffian punched Sparrow square on the jaw, sending her flying through the air. The squaw landed hard on her back where she continued to wail and protest. Her assailant took three long strides and drew back his leg to kick the woman to silence. Before he could deliver the blow, Cutler charged him, swung his lacrosse stick, and broke it over the hulking man's back.

The trader whirled and lashed out with a flurry of wild punches that Will easily dodged. Cutler answered with some jabs of his own, but they bounced off the merchant's biceps as if they were made of iron. The scoundrel then whacked Will with a mighty clout that about knocked his head from his neck. With his ears ringing from the blow, Big Cat snatched a musket from one of the gawking brave's hands and swung the butt end of it at his opponent's knee. It hit with a fearful crunch, and the stocky brawler collapsed as if struck by a felled hemlock.

Mac, meanwhile, grabbed the second musket and pointed it meaningfully at the other scruffy rascal, who had drawn a hatchet during the confusion of Will's fight. With a menacing growl, the Scotchman said, "Don't even think on it, mister. Ye best help up your henchman and git a goin' before Big Cat really gets riled."

Fixing Will with a hateful leer, the whipped trader lurched to his feet. Then, he wiped his hands on his stained smock and slammed his busted tri-corner hat on his head. Spitting tobacco juice to accent his words, he snarled, "You ain't seen the last o' us. You can bet on it!"

"Ye can also bet ye won't be sellin' this rum to another village," snapped Alex, knocking a hole in the side of the wooden keg with the rifle butt.

Roaring like an enraged bruin, the merchant hobbled furiously to his horse and yanked a pistol from a holster slung over the saddle horn. Before he could discharge the weapon, Lightnin', Bearbite, and Dark Thunder stormed through the gate and surrounded him in an instant. Looking down the wrong end of three rifle barrels, the trader tossed aside his pistol, crawled on his mount, and galloped out of the village in a cloud of choking dust.

The departed man's partner stared fearfully at the mountain men and warrior chief and then stammered, "C-C-Can I go, too?"

"Aye," rumbled MacDonald, "an' don't a ever come back!"

To make sure the rascal did leave, Will and his friends roughly escorted him out of the village. When they arrived at the trail leading south, Mac stampeded the trader's pack horses and then speeded the fellow after them with a kick in the pants. The trader snarled something under his breath before sprinting off to catch his bolting animals.

With a jubilant cheer, the mountain men returned to Ishua Town. As they reentered the gate, they found Sparrow waiting for them. The woman motioned for Will to approach her. Reluctantly, he shuffled to her side, and she began measuring him with a long chord with knots tied in it at regular intervals. When Cutler pulled away in alarm, the squaw babbled, "No hurt. No hurt. I fit you. For wedding."

"Thank God," whistled Hawkins with an exaggerated look of horror. "I figgered fer sure you was measurin' 'im fer grave clothes."

"It's the same thing if he's gettin' hitched," cackled Bearbite. "Congratulations, Big Cat!"

Sparrow continued to stretch her chord over Will's body until she knew the length of his arms and legs and the thickness of his torso. Afterward, she gave his hand a heartfelt squeeze and scurried off to join a jabbering circle of squaws.

In the next instant a beaming Bright Star burst from the Bear clan longhouse carrying an empty clay pot. She was humming a sweet melody that made Cutler forget his friends were standing next to him. The lad felt a lump form in his throat as he watched her wiggle toward him. Smiling up into Will's face, the princess invited, "Come with me to river."

Cutler hooked his arm through Bright Star's, and they meandered off through the town gates. The sunshine created an aura around their faces as they exchanged happy smiles. Once they were out of sight of the village, Will pulled the girl close and bent to kiss her pouty lips. She pretended to resist before embracing him with the whole heat of her passion. By the time she stepped away, the lad so quivered with emotion that the princess said, "We better go on. Mother need water to prepare wedding food. There is always tomorrow."

"Yes, tomorrow," echoed Will, following her down the path to the shimmering river.

The next morning the whole village gathered for Will and Bright Star's wedding ceremony.

Dressed in white rabbit fur and leather, the happy couple stood before Dark Thunder, who held the sanction to perform the most significant Iroquois ritual. After smiling approvingly at his daughter and Cutler, the chief solemnly intoned, "Marriage is a great commitment before the Creator. Bright Star. Will. You must promise to nurture and respect one another in your lifetime together. I am honored to unite you as one being."

As the sachem's words faded away, the Iroquois men, accompanied by gourd rattles and water drums, began chanting a lively song. This initiated the Rabbit Dance led by the newlyweds and joined by other well-wishing couples. Bright Star's face beamed with joy when Will held her close and whirled her around and around, totally oblivious to anyone but his new bride.

After the beating drums grew silent, everyone rushed to log tables heaped with corn bread, roast venison, and an assortment of cooked game. Wolfing down a huge hunk of bear meat, Hawkins said between bites, "It's almost trappin' season, ain't it, boys?"

"Aye," replied MacDonald, "but I hear that the Delawares will make it mighty hot for any white man venturin' into the Alleghenies."

"Well, I reckon I'd rather take my chances with them rascals than hang around here," mumbled Bob. "Ain't you seen how Bear Woman's been eyin' me since Sparrow took Will as her son-in-law?"

"Come on, Mac, ya must hear the fall winds a callin'," prodded Lightnin'.

"Unfortunately, I do," sighed Alex. "We best not leave, though, before givin' the young folks their gifts."

At that moment Will and Bright Star broke free from the mob of well-wishers and rushed over to the three mountain men to exchange smiles. The trappers vigorously shook hands with their young partner and repeatedly hugged the bride until she giggled from all their attention. Afterward, Jack said, "Will, you an' yer beautiful wife are gonna need a few things to git started. Take these horns o' black powder that musta fell off them traders' horses yestiddy. There's enough here to kill plenty o' deer fer you an' the whole bear clan."

"Aye, an' please accept this plaid cloth I been luggin' with me for many a year," added MacDonald. "It's wool I brung all the way from Scotland an' will make warm blankets for your bairns when they commence to comin'."

"I got somethin' fer ya, too," chortled Bear-bite. "It's them gold sovereigns that I happened across after Braddock's redcoats got whopped. Now, dad gum it! Let's git out o' here, boys, before Bear Woman makes me a set o' them rabbit skin clothes."

# BIBLIOGRAPHY

Axtell, James. The European and the Indian: Essays in the Ethnohistory of Colonial North America. Oxford: Oxford University Press, 1981.

"Batteau Fact Sheet," <http://www.nysm.nysed.gov/batteau/> (2 January 2008).

"Battle of Culloden," <http://en.wikipedia.org/wiki/Battle_of_Culloden> (17 November 2007).

Ben Bowie and His Mountain Men. New York: Dell Publishing Company, Feb.-April 1958.

Best of the Backwoodsman. Westcliffe, CO: Backwoodsman Press, 1984.

Borneman, Walter R. The French & Indian War: Deciding the Fate of North America. New York: HarperCollins Publishers, 2006.

Bruchac, Joseph. "A Mohawk Village in 1491: Otstungo," National Geographic, October 1991, pp. 68-82.

"Clan/Family Histories—MacDonald/Donald/MacDonnell," <http://www.rampantscotland.com/clans/blclan macdonald.htm> (19 November 2007).

"Clarion River," <http://en.wikipedia.org/wiki/Clarion_River> (2 December 2007).

"Clothing Requirements," www.marinesducontrecoeur.org (6 January 2008).

"Culloden Moor and the Story of the Battle: Chapter VI," <http://www.queenofscots.co.uk/culloden/cullch6.html> (17 November 2007).

Doane, Nancy Locke. Indian Doctor. Charlotte, NC: Aerial Photographic Service, Inc.

Douglas, Ronald Macdonald. Scottish Lore and Folklore. New York: Beekman House, 1982.

Ferree Family Gunsmiths," <http://www.ferreereunion.com/gunsmiths.htm> (17 December 2007).

Fisher, Vardis. Mountain Man. Moscow, ID: University of Idaho Press, 1965.

"French and Indian War—Uniform Chart for French Regiments," <http:www.warof1812.ca/charts/7war chtf.htm> (1 January 2008).

Garbino, William. Along the Allegheny. Midway, PA: Midway Publishing, 2005.

"Haudenosaunee: Women's Clothing," <http://www.peace4 turtleisland.org/pages/womensclothing.htm> (18 February 2008).

"Haudenosaunee: Women's Headwear," <http://www.peace 4turtleisland.org/pages/womensheadwear.htm> (18 February 2008).

Kirkland, Turner E. Dixie Gun Work, Inc. Arms Catalogue. Union City, TN, 2004.

Kanatiiosh. "Creator's Game," <http://www.peace4turtle island.org/pages/creatorsgame.htm> (1 Sept. 2000).

Kanatiiosh. "Lacrosse: How to Play the Game and How Sticks Are Made," <http://www.peace4turtleisland. org/pages/lacrosseplayed.htm> (May 2001).

Laycock, George. The Mountain Men. Guilford, CT: The Lyons Press, 1996.

Lofano, Michael A. Daniel Boone: An American Life. Lexington, KY: University of Kentucky Press, 2003.

"MacDonald History," <http://www.scotclans.com/scottish_
clans/clan_macdonald/history.html> (19 November
2007).

McCafferty, Keith. "Primitive Survival Skills." Field &
Stream, February 2006, pp. 49-59.

"Mohawk Marriage," <http://en.wikipedia.org/wiki/
Mohawk_nation> (10 February 2008).

Mollo, John. Uniforms of the American Revolution. New
York: Macmillan Publishing Co., Inc., 1975.

Montgomery, David. Mountainman Crafts & Skills.
Guilford, CT: The Lyons Press, 2000.

"Native American Houses," <http://www.warof1812.ca/
charts/7warchtf.htm> (1 January 2008).

"Ottawa Indian Fact Sheet," <http://www.geocities.com/
bigorrin/ottawa_kids.htm> (13 December 2007).

"Ottawa Indians," <http://www.ohiohistorycentral.org/
entry.php?rec=614> (13 December 2007).

Richmond, Betty H. Young George Washington: Frontier
Spy. Cochranton, PA: Specialty Group Printing of
Crawford County, 2003.

"Shawnee Men," <http://www.turtletrack.org/Issues02/
co_05182002_Re...> (18 May 2002).

Sipe, C. Hale. The Indian Wars of Pennsylvania.
Lewisburg, PA: Wennawoods Publishing, 2006.

Smail, Larry A. The Attack on Kit-Han-Ne Kittaning
Pennsylvania September 8, 1756. Chicora, PA:
Mechling Bookbindery, 2006.

Smith, Thomas Price. James Smith, Frontier Patriot.
Victoria, B.C.: Trafford Publishing, 2003.

"Story of the Pennsylvania Rifle," <http://ourancestry.com/
rifle.html> (17 December 2007).

Waldman, Carl. <u>Atlas of the North American Indian</u>. New York: Checkmark Books, 2000.

Way, Frederick, Jr. <u>The Allegheny</u>. New York: Farrar & Rinehart, 1942.

Wellman, Paul I. <u>Indian Wars and Warriors East</u>. Cambridge, MA: The Riverside Press, 1959.

# AUTHOR PROFILE:
## WILLIAM P. ROBERTSON

William P. Robertson was born and raised in the wilds of Pennsylvania and has been an avid woodsman since his youth. He first read of the exploits of the Eastern mountain men in the Ben Bowie comic books of the late 1950's. His father, Paul, rewarded him with these comics if he sat still for their old Italian barber when getting his brushcut. Soon, Bill was reading the biographies of all the Indians and pioneers he could borrow from Lincoln Elementary School in Bradford, PA. Some of his favorite tales were of Dan Morgan, Davy Crockett, and Black Hawk, the Sac chief. He also begged his parents to buy him Paul I. Wellman's wonderful book, <u>Indian Wars and Warriors East</u>. These stories, along with Bill's own deer hunting and native brook trout fishing adventures, served as the inspiration for <u>Ambush in the Alleghenies</u>. The author now hopes to have more fun as a French and Indian War reenactor. Below, he is dressed as a woodsman of the 1750's. And, yes, Bill did own a coonskin cap when he was a boy.

# AUTHOR PROFILE:
# DAVID RIMER

Currently retired, David Rimer taught speech and English for thirty-four years at Bradford Area High School in Bradford, PA. He received his BS degree from Clarion University, an MEd from Edinboro University, and further graduate credits from St. Bonaventure, Gannon University, and East Stroudsburg University. David and his wife, Marcia, live in Bradford, PA. They have one daughter, Stephanie, who is a public school librarian. Mr. Rimer has edited several books for Robyl Press and is a published mystery author. He began collaborating with William P. Robertson in 1989 and co-wrote the Bucktail novel series about the famous Civil War sharpshooters, the First Pennsylvania Rifles. Robertson and Rimer's book, The Bucktails at the Devil's Den, was a finalist in the Best Books 2007 Awards sponsored by USABookNews.com.

# THE BUCKTAIL NOVEL SERIES

William P. Robertson and David Rimer have also collaborated on a seven-novel series about the famous Civil War rifle regiment—the Bucktails. Acting as skirmishers for the Union Army, these Pennsylvania sharpshooters were the equivalent of today's Army Rangers.

The books trace the adventures of two frontier lads who stand the test of fire at Dranesville, Antietam, Gettysburg, and the Wilderness. Also detailed are the brutal marches, lousy rations, inept generals, and fearful diseases that made survival a true test of courage for these young riflemen.

Robertson and Rimer create historical fiction that's loaded with action and as hard-hitting as the Civil War itself. Although the books are geared toward middle school students, many adults have enjoyed them, too. For excerpts and cover photos of the seven novels listed below, visit Bill's website at http://bucktailsandbroomsticks.com.

**From White Mane Publishing**:
Hayfoot, Strawfoot: The Bucktail Recruits
The Bucktails' Shenandoah March
The Bucktails' Antietam Trials
The Battling Bucktails at Fredericksburg

**From Infinity Publishing**:
The Bucktails: Perils on the Peninsula
The Bucktails at the Devil's Den
The Bucktails' Last Call

Autographed copies of the Bucktail novels may be ordered directly from the authors at P.O. Box 293, Duke Center, PA 16729-0293. The White Mane titles are $11 each postpaid. The Infinity titles are $15 each postpaid. Order all seven books for the discount price of $75. Make checks payable to Bill Robertson.

# GLOSSARY

Alleghenies—Mountainous wilderness that stretches across western end of present-day Pennsylvania.

Brown Bess—Smoothbore flintlock musket used by British army in the French and Indian War. It was only accurate up to 80 yards.

Culloden—Battle in which Scottish Jacobite forces were brutally defeated by English under the Duke of Cumberland. Occurring on April 16, 1746, it was last battle fought on mainland Britain.

Double Set Trigger—Two triggers on a rifle. One acts as a safety. The other fires rifle.

Flintlock—Black powder rifle that employs a hammer holding a flint. When trigger is squeezed, cocked hammer falls, strikes the frizzen, and creates a spark that ignites priming powder poured in the pan.

Forks of the Ohio—Point of land where the Allegheny and Monongahela Rivers come together to form the Ohio River. The French built Fort Duquesne here at present-day Pittsburgh, Pennsylvania.

Gauntlet—Double file of Indians facing each other and armed with clubs, switches, and axes with which to strike a captive who is forced to run between them.

Indentured Servant—Person who agrees to work for another for a specified time in exchange for his travel and living expenses. Many Scottish immigrants used this arrangement to come to America.

Logstown—Indian village and trading center where the Iroquois Half-King lived. It was located on the Ohio River.

Longhouse—House of over a hundred feet in length made of a wooden frame and covered with elm bark. This was main dwelling used by Iroquois tribe.

Medicine—Scent used to attract beaver to the long spring trap employed by mountain men.

Ohio Company—Virginia land speculators who attempt trade and settlement in territory of Ohio Valley also claimed by the French.

Pennsylvania Long Rifle—Rifled flintlock musket used by the hunters and trappers of the Alleghenies. It was accurate up to 300 yards.

Possibles Bag—Bag with a shoulder strap used by hunters to carry their shooting supplies, trail food, and personal items.

Ring Hunt—Indians set a circle of grass on fire to drive hiding game out into the open.

Sachem—An Indian chief.

Scalp—War trophy taken by Indians who cut the hair from the crown of an enemy's head as proof of their kill. Showed warrior's power and bravery.

Scalp Lock—A strip of hair on the crown of the otherwise shaved head of an Indian warrior. Also known as Mohawk Haircut.

Speech Belt—Wampum belt made of beads that Indians used to send messages to one another.

Walking Purchase—1737 treaty between Pennsylvania and the Delaware tribe. Government was to receive all the Indian land that could be walked in a day and a half. The Delawares were cheated when fast-walking colonial athletes were employed.

Wigwam—Domed dwelling made of a pole frame covered with bark, woven mats or animal skins.

Will's Creek—Town in Maryland serving as base of operations for the Ohio Company. Also known as Fort Cumberland.

# CHARACTERS (In Their Order of Appearance)

Robert Dinwiddie—Governor of the British colony of Virginia.

George Washington—Officer of the Virginia militia.

Christopher Gist—Frontiersman and Ohio Company guide.

Lightnin' Jack Hawkins—Mountain man and fur trapper known for his quickness.

Alexander MacDonald—Hawkins' Scottish partner known for his sour disposition.

Captain Joncaire—French commander stationed at Venango.

Bold Wolf—Villainous Ottawa chief who wants to kill all English like one pigeon.

Will Cutler—Young trapper nicknamed "Big Cat." He's skilled with all kinds of weapons.

Bearbite Bob Winslow—Experienced old mountain man known for his illusiveness, courage, and trapping abilities.

John Frazer—English trader who gets burned out by the French.

Deep Waters—Treacherous Shawnee chief.

Jacob Van Braam—Washington's French interpreter who misunderstands the terms of surrender at Fort Necessity.

Tanacharison—Iroquois Half-King who rules over the subjugated tribes in the Ohio Valley.

Bear Woman—Bearbite Bob's Iroquois girlfriend.

Bright Star—The Iroquois princess Will Cutler marries.

Dark Thunder—An Iroquois sachem and father of Bright Star.

Thomas Jones—A trader stationed at Will's Creek, the Ohio Company's base of operations.

Captain Contrecoeur—Captured the Forks of the Ohio for the French and erected Fort Duquesne.

Sieur De Jumonville—French commander killed during George Washington's first victory near Fort Necessity. French accuse Washington of assassinating Jumonville.

M. DeVilliers—French officer who forces Washington to surrender at Fort Necessity.

George Croghan—Indian trader and scout. He was in Braddock's advance party when it encountered French forces.

Scarouady—Chief who led Iroquois after the Half-King dies.

Edward Braddock—Arrogant British general, known as "Bulldog," who led the disastrous campaign against Fort Duquesne.

Sergeant Wood—Grenadier who assaults Bright Star at Fort Cumberland.

Colonel Thomas Gage—Led Braddock's advance force against Fort Duquesne.

Colonel Burton—Organized the English rearguard after Braddock's defeat.

Dr. Craik—British physician who tended Braddock's wounds.

Sparrow—Bright Star's mother.

CPSIA information can be obtained at www.ICGtesting.com
Printed in the USA
BVOW11s1327090914

365978BV00013B/236/P